The Golden Gryphon Feather

The Kaphtu Trilogy – Book One

By

Richard Purtill

ISBN: 1-4107-1337-7 (e-book)
ISBN: 1-4107-1338-5 (Paperback)

This book is printed on acid free paper.

Original edition published by DAW Books

Cover art and illustration by George Barr.

1stBooks - rev. 02/07/03

For more about the Kaphtu Trilogy and other works by
Richard Purtill, visit our official website at
alivingdog.com

To
Homer
First and greatest
teller of tales of fantasy
this book is dedicated.

Chapter One: THE SHIP

I first saw the land of Kaphtu from the deck of one of the sea king's ships. When we made the landfall I was sitting, as usual, in the little shelter on the stern of the ship, with the captain and the off-duty steersman. The other six girls were sitting under the shelter amidships, chattering and combing their hair, and the boys were in the bow oiling their bodies and doing what exercises they could in the restricted space. I knew that if I joined the girls the chatter would fade away to an uneasy silence and the ugly word "traitor" would hover unspoken in the air. No female, of course, would be welcome in the little masculine group at the bow, but if any of them did notice me it would be with a black look or a scowl.

It had all started innocently enough. The first day out from Phaleron we had all huddled together amidships while the crew labored at the oars, and when we moored that night near the sea god's temple at Sunion all of us were too tired and dazed to talk much. But as soon as we got beyond the Cape the next day the oars were shipped and the sail was raised, for there was a hard, steady wind from the North. The farther we got from land the higher the seas rose and the more violently the ship moved. Every summer since I was a child I had sailed to my mother's home on the island of Aegina and I can never remember having been seasick. Soon I was the only Athenian not lying in the bottom of the ship and moaning or else hanging miserably over the side. Soon after that the men who were our guards and their captain were moaning and retching along with their charges and the crew and I were left to enjoy the dazzling sun and the steady wind which blew away its heat, the sparkling waves and the exhilarating plunging of the ship.

As I knew from my voyages to Aegina, sailors not only admire a novice who is not seasick, they treat the person with a touch of awe. To be free of seasickness means that you have the blood of some god, probably a sea god, and anyone close to the gods is a person to keep on the good side of. So, as on previous voyages, I soon became a mascot with the crew, free to roam all over the ship and talk to anyone who was not busy with some task that interfered with talking. The difference between this voyage and my voyages to Aegina was my overwhelming need to know all I could of our destination and what awaited us there. I spent little time with the friendly sailors who only spoke a few words of Danaan and a great deal of time with the captain, who spoke it as well as I did, plying him with questions about his language and his country.

I was fortunate in two ways. The officers of the sea king's ships are the captain, the sailing master and the steersman. Ordinarily each has his own apprentice and the six form a tight little group that does not welcome outsiders. But on our ship the group was not so tightly knit. The sailing master was a grizzled, silent man whose apprentice was his younger brother, equally grizzled and equally silent. The two spent most of their time together, checking the sail or playing complex and interminable games. The steersman was a gentle, friendly old man who left most of the handling of the steering oar to his apprentice, a nephew, who was young and shy. And by what turned out to be a stroke of luck for me the captain's apprentice, his oldest son, had broken his arm just before the ship sailed and the ship had sailed without him. Thus there was an empty stool in the little stern shelter and an empty place that I little by little began to fill.

But I was luckiest of all in the fate that sent P'sero as the captain on this voyage. Physically he was quite unlike my father, being short, dark and lithe, whereas my father has reddish hair and is tall, lanky and clumsy in matters not related to his work. But like my father P'sero was a complete master of his chosen trade and like my father he treated me simply as a person, not as a child, though I blush now when I think how childish I still was, not as a member of a dangerous and alien sex, but simply as a person.

In this P'sero was unlike even most of his fellow Kaphtui. No proper Danaan male, of course, regards a woman as an equal or even as fully a person. In Kaphtu women have respect but it is a respect mingled with fear. No man of Kaphtu forgets that the Mother is older than the Kings or that his land was once ruled by women. But P'sero and my father both looked at men and women, old and young, as people, to be liked and respected if they deserved to be, not judged by their age or sex. So I soon slipped into very much the same relation with P'sero that I had with my father. The other officers took their lead from him and this little interval between my old life and my new one was cushioned for me; from being the daughter of my father's house, I became for a little while the youngest of P'sero's little family afloat.

At first my compatriots were in no condition to notice. P'sero drove the ship mercilessly, taking full advantage of the favorable wind. He did not moor the ship until the light began to fade and if the wind had not died down at dusk he would have sailed by night, inconceivable as that would seem to mainland sailors. When we moored even the crew was grateful enough to eat a little food and tumble into sleep. Bracing yourself against the plunging of the ship was almost as tiring as walking all day. But seasickness does not last forever and as my companions began to sit up and take notice the first thing they noticed was me, trying out my growing stock of Kaphtui words on the sailors or sitting at P'sero's feet holding long conversations. At first these were in Danaan, but since our major topic of conversation was Kaphtu, he began to slip more and more often into his native tongue and by the end of the voyage although I will not say I was speaking Kaphtui, I was certainly not speaking Danaan.

To the others it seemed that I had simply gone over to our captors' side. When the guards got over their own seasickness they took their cue from the crew and I was soon chattering with them as freely as with the sailors. The chatter was mostly composed of commonplaces about wind and sea and the laughter was mainly at my mistakes in using their language, but to the other Athenians I seemed to be currying favor with the enemy. There were spiteful remarks which I was meant to overhear when I lay down to sleep near the other girls, and toward the end of the voyage one of the boys tried to warn me away from associating with the Kaphtui.

He was a tall, dark boy with a big nose; his name was Euphoros and he gave himself airs among us because he was the son of one of the concubines of someone fairly important on the Hill. At times I still found it useful to act younger and more innocent than I actually was, and I simply looked at him wide-eyed and said: "But I'm learning their language. Don't you want us to be able to deal with people there when we reach the end of the voyage?" If I had been defiant, he might have blustered, but he had no answer for childish reasonableness, and the reminder that the voyage would soon end aroused his fears. I had no idea then how terrified the others were. So Euphoros merely muttered something about being too friendly and stamped off, his dignified departure marred by a frantic grab at the side as the ship hit a larger wave. I'm afraid that I just laughed and forgot him.

But the result was that the others decided to ignore me as being either an idiot or a traitor, so the division between myself and the other Athenians became even wider. When the shining peaks of the Great Ones were spotted by the lookout and the crew raised a cheer for the landfall, I cheered and laughed with them feeling foolishly as if I were coming home, while the other Athenians looked glumly at each other or stared at the deck at their feet, dreading what the landing would bring.

They must have passed a miserable night, knowing that we had arrived and having no idea of what was ahead. For we did not make port that night. We had moored the night before at the most southerly moorage of the Circle Islands, hardly more than a great rock half awash in the sea. Now as the sun set and the wind still blew steadily the dark outline of Kaphtu ahead of us seemed to get no nearer. It was fully dark when we came near enough to shore to throw out our anchors, rowing in since the wind had died.

It had been eerie coming in in the dark with the oars stilled periodically so that P'sero could judge our distance from shore by the sound of the waves, but morning found us securely anchored in a shallow bay fringed with rocky cliffs. We rowed out from shore in the cold light of dawn, getting sea room before the winds pinned us to the shore, but we did not put up our sail and only a few men stayed at the oars while the rest began a thorough cleaning and refurbishing of the ship. The shelters astern and amidships were taken down and stored away, and the captain's high-backed chair stood alone in the middle of the afterdeck. P'sero emerged from below in a richly embroidered kilt, with his elaborately decorated belt cinched even tighter than usual. Even the oarsmen brought out clean kilts and decorated belts from caches under their benches.

I was still childish enough to be carried away by this dressing up and got a friendly oarsman to carry up my chest from the hold. It was the battered wooden chest with metal studs which had stood at the foot of

my father's bed ever since I remembered, and for a
moment looking at it I had a sharp pang of
homesickness, but I was soon distracted. The big
oarsman looked at the ropes which secured the chest
and poked a finger at the knot. "A seaman tied that,"
he said.

But my father had tied it, and he was no seaman—
or was he? I suddenly realized how little I knew of my
father's life before I had been born. He was never one
to tell stories about himself. For the moment I had
other things to think of. I untied the intricate knot and
opened the lid of the chest, wondering for the first time
what my father had found to fill It. I was wearing my
summer dress. Like most dresses in Athens it was a
folded piece of cloth pinned together at the shoulders
and belted at the waist with a cord. It was already too
short for me, and I should have spent last winter at my
mother's loom weaving a new one. My winter dress
was still long enough, but it was shabby, and would be
too heavy anyhow. Did I have anything in this chest to
change to?

I need not have feared. My winter cloak was on
top, but under it was a beautiful piece of material; one
of my mothers dresses. As a child I had always thought
my mother'. clothing finer than that of any other
woman and I saw now that memory had not deceived
me: the material was the finest, smoothest and lightest
I had ever seen. One more mystery concerning my
enigmatic mother, but I had no time for that now
either. I found a cord with a golden sheen and a pair of
sandals which seemed to have gilded edges. Tucked in
a corner was a gift my father had given me last year:

two shoulder pins with heads formed like the little blue wild flowers which were my favorites.

I stood up clutching my finery. My friend the oarsman grinned and jerked his head toward the space below the afterdeck. 'Throw up your old dress," he said. "I'll pack it and cord the chest again. I think I can do that knot." I ducked below and emerged in my mother's dress to find that the men were already back at their oars and the ship was under way. My chest was sitting, tied up again, beside the captain's chair and P'sero gestured for me to use it as a seat. The stools were cleared away; the steersman stood by the steering oar and the two brothers were supervising the breaking out of the sail.

The other Athenians were sitting on the deck amidships, the boys still a little separate from the girls. The guards were undergoing some sort of inspection from their captain, but he paused and glanced in my direction. P'sero turned to me. "Tell your friends that we will soon be in port. Reassure them, if you can. Then come back to me." He spoke loudly enough for the captain to hear and that settled any ideas that the guard captain may have had of herding me in with the others.

As the Kaphtui say, "On board his ship, the captain is M'nos."

That is a double-edged saying like most Kaphtu sayings. "M'nos" means "king of the sailors," and the throne of the king of Kaphtu is a captain's chair like the one P'sero sat on now.

I made my way over to the other Athenians, looking for a friendly face. None of the girls would meet my eyes and Euphoros turned away, but a stocky boy with gray eyes rose from his place and came toward me.

"I am Glaukos," he said and then stopped uncertainly. I smiled at him a little too broadly out of relief; he probably thought I was a fool.

But I had no time to worry about that now. "Tell the others," I said loudly enough to make the telling unnecessary, "that we will be in port soon." I tried to remember what I had picked up from conversations during the last few days. "We'll walk from the port to the king's palace; it's about as far inland from the port as Athens is from Phaleron. I've learned a good deal about why we were brought here, but it's too complicated to explain now. We're not going to be killed and we're not going to be enslaved, so don't act like slaves or condemned criminals. You'll certainly be stared at, but don't assume that you're being jeered at. Even if you are, ignore it. Remember that you're Athenians."

His look was puzzled but not hostile. "We thought that you'd forgotten that."

I met his eyes. "I haven't," I said shortly. It seemed a good finish to our conversation, so I turned and went back to Captain P'sero. The young apprentice steersman was standing beside him holding a miniature of one of the ship's oars about half again as tall as a man, stained a rich red-purple and beautifully polished. P'sero took it from him and handed It to me.

"As we enter the port will you stand beside me and hold the oar, so?" He rested the butt against his right foot and held the blade upright at a slight angle.

Something in his manner told me that I was being given a post of honor and I took the oar from him as solemnly and ceremoniously as I could. The apprentice turned away, looking a little disappointed, and took his place behind the steersman.

Standing beside the captain, I could see under the bottom edge of the sail that we were nearing the shore, and that the whole curve of the shallow bay was crowded with houses, coming almost to the shore. There seemed to be a sort of wall or platform in front of the houses and in front of this ships were moored, more ships and larger ships than I had ever seen in Phaleron. We seemed to be headed right for the wall and the ships under full sail, but the two brothers were standing tensely by the ropes which controlled the sail.

P'sero's voice was quite calm and unmoved. "This is Amnisos. Look just to the left of the mast. My house is there; the third row up. I hope to welcome you there before too long."

The thought of meeting P'sero's wife and children, all of whom he had proudly described to me, steadied me, which is what he probably intended, and I stood up a little straighter.

"Now," said P'sero in a quiet tone that nevertheless could be heard all over the ship. The brothers released the ropes which held the bottom of the sail just enough to spill the wind and two teams of seamen hauled at the ropes which brailed the sail so that it was hauled up to cling to the yard in symmetrical swags. Without the force of the wind the ship slowed and with a gentle pressure on the steering oar from the old steersman we headed directly into a niche in the stone wall just wide enough to hold the ship. As we glided in, moving more and more slowly, I could see that the wall was in fact a stone pavement at about the same level as our deck, with rectangular slips in which ships could be moored. The ship almost touched the end of the slip and came to a dead stop. In fact, it would have drifted backwards had not a young man on the dock snubbed a rope around our stern post. His broad grin would have told me his identity even without the bandaged arm. It was P'sero's son N'suto, whose place on board I had taken for awhile. He jumped lightly aboard and I handed over the purple oar to him. His look was pleased but puzzled.

P'sero beamed at us both. "My son, this is the Lady Chryseis."

N'suto, perhaps impressed by his father's tone, gave me the salute that the Kaphtui save for their goddesses and their priestesses; the hand carried to the brow as if to shield the eyes from a dazzling light. His soft voice gave me the title that went with the salute: "Bright Lady."

And that was my welcome to Kaphtu.

Chapter Two: THE HOUSE

After our impressive arrival there was something of an anticlimax. As so often at sea we had hurried only to wait. Because of our late landfall and early start our arrival had come as a surprise and hurried messages had to be sent to those who were to meet us at the dock. N'suto and I wandered over to the side of the ship and chatted quietly as we looked out over the harbor. I soon learned that the purple oar was a great mark of honor, the sign of the best ship and the best captain in the sea king's fleet. N'suto was pleased that I had been the one chosen to hold it, simply because he grudged the honor to any other member of the crew. His jealousy of anyone taking his place as his father's apprentice was probably the reason P'sero had not shipped a replacement when N'suto had broken his arm. The jealousy did not seem to extend to me; as a very temporary and honorary replacement I had not threatened his own position. He was very determined to follow in his father's footsteps and his single-minded interest in ships and the sea might have been tedious if it were not for his youth and enthusiasm.

As he plied me with questions, not about Athens but about the voyage, the dock area around the ship gradually filled with the sailors from other ships, porters, dock officials and the hangers-on one finds in any port. There were some friendly exchanges between our crew and those on shore. The great joke, repeated over and over again as newcomers kept arriving, was the inquiry whether we had intended to sail right on up to N'sos. Our approach to the dock under sail had evidently been something of a feat, but one of a kind expected of the captain who held the purple oar.

The town of Amnisos rose in steps up the low hills behind the harbor and now from the upper reaches of the town a colorful procession came down to the dock. It was composed of women, but such women as I had never seen in Athens, even among the women of the king's court. They were dressed in flounced skirts of many colors and their hair was elaborately dressed in ringlets and long curls. They were bejeweled, painted and perfumed, but the most surprising part of their costume to Athenian eyes were the short-sleeved jackets which they wore, which left their breasts completely exposed. Most of the women formed a little chattering group on the dock, and I could see the Athenian boys staring and the Athenian girls looking nonplussed, as well they might. Our Athenian dresses were white or cream or gray depending on the wool of which they had been woven and were straight and unadorned. The other girls had not even had a chance to change their dresses. We were a drab little group of doves compared to the gaudy plumage of the group on the dock.

Some of the women, including some that looked older but were dressed like the others, had gone over to a small building on the dock that from its decoration seemed to be a shrine.

"Priestesses of the sea goddess," said N'suto in my ear. I must have looked surprised because he grinned and said, "We Kaphtui have a god and a goddess for everything."

I was later to learn how true, and how significant, that was.

The women now emerged from the shrine, moving with a sort of gliding walk and giving a monotonous chant. The leader was carrying a double-headed axe which seemed to be made entirely of gold. She moved majestically over to where P'sero stood waiting at the side of the ship and handed him the axe. He held it by the handle with both hands, held it in front of his eyes, and chanted in turn. He was joined by the sailing master and his brother from the waist of the ship, but their chant went to a different rhythm.

N'suto said in a low voice, "My father is a priest of the sea god; they are priests of the Winds. They are giving thanks for good voyage." P'sero touched the axe to his chest, his forehead and his lips and then touched it to the sternpost of the ship before handing it back to the priestess. The little procession returned to the shrine chanting until they entered the door.

I decided it was time for us Athenians to make our presence felt. I stepped to the edge of the afterdeck and began a rhythmic clapping. When the Athenians' eyes were on me I sang out the first line of the Spring Hymn to Athena. They would all know it, the girls and boys of our year had sung it not long ago at the festival. Glaukos took up the boys' part and the others, carried along by the familiar words and tune, joined in. As the hymn went on they even made some of the movements; the space was not much more restricted than that of the choral area on the Hill.

The Kaphtui on the dock listened respectfully; they are a people who take the gods seriously, though not always solemnly. When we finished our hymn there was a little murmur of approval, almost of applause. P'sero appeared at my elbow. 'That was well done, Chryseis,' he said. "Perhaps better than you know. Now we will go up to the House." He began to call out orders and in a surprisingly short time a little procession had formed. It was led by P'sero, myself and the captain of the guards. The other Athenians followed us in a double line flanked at intervals by the guardsmen. The tail of the procession was made up of porters from the dock carrying our boxes and bundles. Seeing how skimpy some of those bundles were, I wondered again how my father had managed to appear at Phaleron with my box all packed so soon after we had been selected and hustled to the ship. Some of the others had nothing of their own, only a few things pressed into their hands as we went to the ship by sympathetic householders on the way.

The captain of the guard looked unhappy, and I had a shrewd suspicion that this sudden procession with P'sero in charge was not in his orders and that he had expected some official party from the palace to meet us. P'sero on shore was no longer the absolute ruler he had been on his own ship, but it would have taken a bolder man than our captain of guards to stand up to the chief captain of the sea king's fleet without definite orders from higher up.

As soon as we got beyond the narrow, winding street of the port city, we were on the main road to N'sos. From what P'sero had told me in our long talks on board I knew that properly speaking it was Ko N'sos, The Great City, but that no Kaphtui called it anything but N'sos, The City. The road itself was an impressive symbol of the royal power of M'nos the Sea King. It was made of dressed stone, as flat as the floor of a temple or palace and wide enough for four to walk abreast. On each side of it was a graveled strip just as broad as the main road; the few people we met along the early part of the way stepped aside on this and watched us pass. Presently we heard the pounding of feet behind us and the ladies who had met us at the port passed us, carried on chair-like litters. The bearers were jogging along at a good pace; there were relief bearers trotting along behind. We passed no animals except a few donkeys which carried goods rather than riders; these seemed to be confined to the strip alongside the stone road.

The slope was gentle, but by the time we had been walking for awhile in the increasingly hot morning sun some muscles unused on the ship began to complain. I was glad that I had usually managed to swim around the ship every morning before we got underway despite the amusement of the crew and the disgust of my fellow Athenians. A few of the younger sailors had joined me, but seamen do not usually regard the sea as something to play in. I had learned to enjoy swimming from other children during my summers on Aegina.

I looked around the gentle green hills, so different from the rockier hills of home. There was little to see here. We passed a few flocks of sheep and an occasional walker or donkey leader coming from the direction we were going. So the girl standing on the rock watching us caught my attention as soon as we came in sight of her. The rock was a large one that had probably been cleared away when the road was made but had been too heavy to move far, so it was right at the edge of the graveled strip. She was evidently looking out for us and as we came nearer peered intently at us from her vantage point of a few feet above the path.

She was dressed much like the women who had met us at the dock, and she had the sort of loop or knot at the back of her neck which I had learned marked a priestess. Though she looked no older than I, she had the intensely dark hair which can look almost blue in some lights and a proud little beak of a nose. She looked vivid and exciting, the kind of girl who would throw herself completely into whatever she was doing. Ever since my childhood redish-gold hair darkened to a nondescript brown, I have envied this kind of dark good looks, and she looked like a person whom it would be exciting to know better.

There were two extraordinary things about her as she stood there. The first was that she was covered from head to foot with a sort of veil of almost transparent, very fine dark material which floated around her like a cloud. And the second was that no one but me seemed to pay any attention to her at all. As I watched, a man carrying a huge untidy bundle of sticks passed by her so closely that she had to step back to avoid being brushed by the sticks. He didn't even glance at her. The eyes of my companions seemed to pass over her without seeing her.

To test this out I waved a hand in her direction and asked P'sero, "Who is that?"

He glanced in the direction I pointed but his eyes traveled past the rock to the man with the sticks now a little past the rock. "A charcoal burner, Lady. Those little branches make a fine charcoal for starting fires."

I didn't ask again; either he did not see the girl or was pretending not to, and I could not square pretending with what I knew of P'sero. My question drew the girl's attention to me and as we passed the rock she stared at me. Her dark eyes met my gray-green ones and widened with shock and surprise. I restrained the impulse to crane my neck around behind me, and by the time we reached a little rise where I could more naturally look back over the road behind, the rock was empty. The hills were close here and she could have walked into one of the little valleys between them, but the whole incident gave me a strange feeling. I have always been able to trust my eyes and I did not doubt them then, but why had the others not seen her? Where had she gone, and why had she been there in the first place?

These thoughts were driven from my mind as we crossed another rise in the ground. Before us the hills fell away to a broad valley in which there ran a peaceful river. Near the river sprawled the flat-roofed homes of N'sos, and on a hill in the center of the huddle of houses was the tremendous bulk of The

House, the palace of M'nos. It was as if one of the three-storied, flat-roofed houses I had seen in the port city had grown and multiplied like the bubbles on top of a cooking pot. There were vast expanses of flat roof, and a jumble of stairways, pillared porches and broad windows. The roofs were at various levels, pierced with large square open areas which seemed to go down into the building, including one immense open space near the center of the great structure. But it was not many buildings, but one great building, as if the scattered buildings of the Acropolis had been joined into one and then built on down over the slopes of the Hill.

This hill was not as high as ours and the sprawling building, covered and concealed it; even from the bottom of the valley it could never have the heart-stopping grandeur of the Hill of Athens seen from the flat ground below. But it had a different sort of impressiveness with its suggestion of a whole cityful of people in one giant building, its insolent lack of fortifications and defenses. The lesser houses that surrounded it would have made a city larger than Athens, but it was the House itself which was the symbol and capital of the sea king's power.

We made our way down the slopes of the hills toward the buildings. A great causeway crossed a gulley between us and the House, but instead of crossing it we turned into a large building which stood at the entrance to the causeway. Again I think the captain of the guards would have liked to protest, but was faced down by P'sero's calm assumption of authority. Inside the building we entered a large rectangular room with benches around the walls. A covey of chattering servant girls led us to the benches and brought water in pitchers and basins to wash our feet, dusty despite the stone pavement of the road. The servant girls' skirts were shorter and less elaborately flounced than those of the women at the port and they wore no jewels. But aside from that their dress was much the same. The room seemed to be full of them, plump and bustling, and when I looked at the wall and saw a fresco of partridges around the wall I almost laughed out loud. P'sero, who had seated himself beside me, caught my eye and grinned. "Even the girls here call themselves 'the partridges' since that was painted," he murmured.

The frescoes were beautiful work, the finest wall paintings I had ever seen and I longed to go over and examine them more carefully. But now the servant girls brought in little rectangular tables with two legs on one end and a single leg on the other. The single leg was placed close to the bench, between P'sero and myself so that we each had a corner of the table in front of us. The part of the table away from the bench was loaded with small dishes, we only had to reach for what we wanted and bring it to the part of the table in front of us.

I ignored most of the dishes of cooked food and had a piece of hearth-bread and some olives. There were three kinds of olives, one too sour for me but the others both good. The daughter of a craftsman soon becomes a connoisseur of olives, for even the poorest family has an olive tree and can pay for craftsman's work with olives or oil. Then I spotted a dish of the

tiny squid fried in oil which I loved and was attending
to it vigorously when an older woman came up with a
cup of wine which she handed to P'sero. He took a sip
and passed it on to me; a sweet wine very much
watered, but cool and refreshing after our walk. With
her occasional shrieks to the maids the woman who
had brought us our wine seemed to be the housekeeper
in charge of this place; P'sero and I were being treated
as the guests of honor. But all of the Athenians were
being served wine and food, and even our guards were
standing about and drinking from cups. The porters
had evidently waited outside or gone to another room.

I had just finished the last squid in the small dish
when a large dignified woman with the priestess-knot
at her neck appeared at the door of the room. She
slowed down as she came toward us, but I thought she
had been hurrying and was not as calm as she tried to
appear. She addressed P'sero in Kaphtui, ignoring me.
"What game are you playing. P'sero?"

He looked beck at her with his usual unshakable
calm. "No game at all, T'ne," he said. "M'nos sent me
to fetch the Athenians and here they are."

She replied angrily, but with an edge of uncertainty
in her voice, "M'nos is not here. You take too much on
yourself P'sero."

He shrugged, his face giving nothing away. "They
were brought here for the Dance. Take them to the
Mistress of the Dance."

She bit her lip and drummed her fingers on our
table. P'sero looked at her blandly. "The axe has two
blades, T'ne. This is your stroke. Do what you will." I
knew she would follow his suggestion because she had

no better idea of her own. I thought that P'sero on his trading ventures for M'nos probably brought home a good return.

The woman looked at me and asked, not bothering to lower her voice, "Is this their leader?"

P'sero answered in a casual tone, 'This is the best of them," and then flicked me an amused glance. I tried to look as if I didn't know what they were talking about; my knowledge of the language was an advantage it would not do to reveal too casually.

P'sero was a step ahead of me; he turned to me and spoke in slow, careful Danaan, warning me that the woman understood my language whether or not she would speak it to me. "This lady will take charge of you, Chryseis. I must return to Amnisos." This was the name of the port city I remembered, where P'sero lived. If the woman was clever enough she might wonder how I knew that. P'sero stood up and looked down at me. "Go on as you have begun, Chryseis. We will meet again." He strode out of the room, leaving me with the woman.

She drummed her fingers again and then made up her mind. She called to the housekeeper. When the woman came to her she said, "Put them in the guest rooms. The guards will stay." Then she turned to me and said in Danaan, "Come." She did not turn her head as she strode out of the room and across the causeway; if she had she would have seen that as I followed her, the porter with my box picked it up and followed me. He looked rather stout and authoritative for an ordinary porter and I wondered if P'sero was still keeping his eye on me in his own way.

We did not enter the palace but turned right after crossing the causeway onto a gravel path which went between the wall of the palace and the gorge. The palace was only three stories tall where we turned, but the ground fell away as we went along and the wall loomed over us higher and higher. Once, we had to stop when a jet of water leaped out from an opening in the palace wall ahead of us, falling into a stone channel that led to the gulley. After a moment it died to a trickie and we stepped over the channel and went on. I sniffed, but it was clean water and not sewage.

When we came to the corner of the House we did not follow the wall on around, but went diagonally across to what seemed like a little grove of trees, a long spear throw from the wall—I realized it must be the south wall—of the House.

Passing through the trees, which were only a fringe, we found ourselves on a flat field of beaten earth, like a practice field for athletes. The woman who had brought me said, "Here she is," and then, I think, went back the way we had come. But I had no eyes and no thoughts of her. Standing in front of me at the corner of the field was a girl, barefoot and dressed only in a kilt and belt like those worn by the male Kaphtui. It was the girl who had looked at us from the rock and her dark eyes were bright and hostile.

Chapter Three: THE BULL

We stood looking at each other for a long moment and I decided that my usual ability to guess what people were thinking and feeling could not be working, because I felt very strongly not only hostility but fear, and how could this girl who was evidently a person in authority here, fear me, a stranger and a captive? She spoke curtly in Danaan, not quite the tone of a mistress to a slave, but certainly the tone of someone in authority to one far below her. A priestess had spoken to me in that tone once when I wandered into the private precincts of a temple. "What is your name?" she asked.

This was a bad question to start with. I told her the usual half truth, in a tone more hostile than it would have been otherwise. "They call me Chryseis." Then I decided it was silly not to try to make some contact with her and I gave her my best childishly innocent smile. "They say it means 'golden.' My hair was really gold as a child but it's darkened since."

She didn't answer but her next question was a shade less peremptory. "Who are your parents?"

This was again somewhat dangerous ground, but I tried to keep my voice friendly as I replied. "My father is a craftsman." I knew from P'sero that this was a more honored status here than it was at home. "My mother was a priestess."

Religion, as I have said, is always a serious matter to the Kaphtui. Perhaps it was that or perhaps just curiosity, but she asked, "What goddess did she serve?"

She assumed, as I had wanted her too, that my mother was dead. Of course for all I knew that was true, although I didn't believe it. But her question was one I could answer without evasion. "The goddess Aphaea. She is worshiped on Aegina. My mother came from there." I was relaxed now, quite prepared to tell her about Aegina and my summers there. But her next remark hit me like a thunderbolt.

"Britomartis," she said. I must have goggled at her like an idiot, hearing my real name which I had always been told to keep secret. She looked at me strangely as she explained, "That's the name of your Aphaea here in Kaphtu. She is worshiped here too."

Suddenly I felt light-hearted. My real name was the Kaphtui name of the goddess whose temple my mother had served. There would be a temple of the goddess here. My mother was not in Athens, not on Aegina. Could she be here, somewhere in Kaphtu? Was that why my father had seemed, strangely, almost glad when he learned that I was one of those chosen to be sent here? "Good," I said, and "good"

The other girl must have been completely puzzled by my behavior, and she fell back on her catechism. "Do you know why you have been brought here?" she said in a tone more like that of her first question.

I met her eyes and prepared to give her a further shock. "Yes," I said. "To be Dancers Before the Throne."

I had used the Kaphtui words, which were the only name I knew for the Dance and this, together with the fact that I knew at all must have been a considerable shock to her. She concealed her surprise magnificently though, much better than I had done, and merely asked in a scornful tone (with only a slight quaver) "And do you know what that means?"

I considered for a moment, trying to draw together the things that I had learned from many conversations with P'sero and from casual references by the rest of the crew. "It is a way you have of worshiping the sea god. The young men and women dance before your king and queen and a great bull is part of the dance. You leap over his horns and roll under his hoofs. It is dangerous, of course, but the god is not pleased if anyone is hurt or killed. If you are the Mistress of The Dance you must be Ariadne, the king's daughter. They say your Dancers are the most skillful that anyone now alive has seen."

I had not meant to flatter her, I was only putting together things I had been told. Because she could see that, she was pleased as she never would be by flattery. But she was outraged too; she must have felt that it was her place to tell me all this, not my place to tell her. She reacted, as I was to learn she often did when annoyed or puzzled, into action. "You know the words; you know nothing of the thing. Look!" She gave a high whistle and lifted an arm.

From the far end of the field six girls and seven
boys, all barefoot and clad in nothing but kilts and
belts ran lightly onto the field. They formed a long
double line extending about halfway from the end of
the field to where we stood. Then from the same gap in
the trees from which they had appeared came two
stocky, powerful men holding ropes which were
twisted around the horns of the biggest bull I had ever
seen. Ariadne stepped to the center of the field at our
end and raised her arm again. The men whipped the
ropes off the bull's horns and it started at a shambling
trot toward Ariadne.

As it passed the first boy, who was standing on a
little hump of ground, he vaulted clear over its back
without touching it. The bull paid no attention to him.
Then first a girl and then a boy, from opposite sides of
the bull's path, did handsprings over the bull, their
hands resting for a second on his back as they went
over. The bull shook his head and his stride
lengthened. A boy threw himself in a sort of
somersault and roll under the bull's feet, passing under
the great belly after the forelegs had passed and before
the back legs came forward. Two girls from opposite
sides ran toward the bull, grabbed his horns and swung
on them. With the swing they gave a twist that brought
them out wide of the bull's flanks; they released the
horns and finished with a tumbler's roll.

As the bull's rush was slowed by this maneuver,
Ariadne ran lightly straight at the bull's head. Her
hands grasped the horns near their base, and as the bull
brought his head back with a mighty toss her body
went with it. Her back fantastically arched, she went

over the bull's head. Her feet touched his broad back and she continued her motion into a handspring from the bull's rump to the ground. One of the boys stepped out of the line and as she came upright touched her hands with his as if to steady her.

The bull now had nothing in front of him but trees; he slowed, skidded and turned back the way he had come. As he galloped, now, down the same path Ariadne and the boy who had caught her hands did simultaneous bandsprings over his back. For a second as their hurtling bodies passed each other they were perpendicular to the bull's back, perfectly in line. A boy who had not jumped before did a handspring on the ground as the bull passed by him, getting enough height so that he was able to touch the bull's back with his feet and continue in a roll in the air which landed him on his feet again, steadied by one of the girls. In terms of sheer strength it was the hardest of the leaps, and it was the last; the bull galloped on out through the gap in the trees and did not reappear.

The other Dancers filed out after the bull and Ariadne walked toward me controlling her breathing admirably, but with an effort. Before she could speak I burst out, "It was beautiful!" I started to say that it was the most thrilling thing I had ever seen, but remembering its religious aspect I said instead, "It is worthy of the god."

My admiration was obviously genuine and Ariadne said almost shyly. "Would you like to do it?"

I was carried away with excitement and asked eagerly, "Can I try? Now?"

She looked startled; this had not been what she meant, but she looked at me consideringly and nodded. "There are some clean kilts on the bush there." I slipped heedlessly out of my mother's dress and sandals and put on the kilt. A piece reinforced with leather passed between my legs, and the two other corners of the triangular piece of cloth wrapped around the waist. The cloth was tucked, but held mostly by the belt; the only one there was plain and worn but the decorative studs were silver. I didn't attempt to cinch the belt as tight as the Kaphtui did.

"I'll guide the bull. Try a side leap," said Ariadne.

As I went to the point on the side she indicated I began to realize what I had let myself in for. My mother had encouraged me to run, jump and tumble, and I could probably still do a vault or even a handspring over a stationary object as high as the bull. But increasingly over the last year or so I had been forced into the mold of an ordinary Athenian woman, unable to run or jump near home, discouraged from going off by myself. Not by my father, of course, but sometimes it seemed that every neighbor, especially the women, were in a conspiracy to make me behave as they thought proper. It was, I now realized, the main reason I had not been unhappier to leave home.

As I stood waiting for the bull to thunder past I wondered how much agility the last year or so had cost me. Still my body had always done what I required of it when it had to, and I was determined not to fail. From the time of Ariadne's signal till the bull was passing me seemed only a second, but then time seemed to slow; the bull was only a large object, softer than stone walls I had vaulted and I did a perfect handspring over his back. My hands were on his back only a second but long enough to give me a slight twist, and I did not land quite straight. But it had been deceptively easy—beginner's luck—and I was mad with excitement and drunk with the smell of the bull which had filled my nostrils as I went over and was still on my hands.

I did not see how Ariadne turned the bull—she did not leap it herself—but it was on its way back and I steadied myself for another try. But just as the bull's head was almost even with me there was a sudden crash. Something had been thrown right into the path of the charging bull—I learned later that it was a clay pot full of burning coals. The bull skidded, bellowed and the wicked horns arced within inches of me. I was set for my leap but had not leapt and instinctively I did the best thing I could have done; grabbed hard at the nearest horn and dragged on it with all my weight. I was dragged over the ground twice and lifted off my feet once, but while I clung to that horn the bull could not gore me.

Before I could even wonder what to do Ariadne was clinging to the other horn and trying to make soothing noises between gasps. Our combined weight was a drag on even those mighty muscles and the bull, of course, was used to being played. His indignation at the crash and the few hot coals which had touched him gradually subsided, and eventually he stood between us quivering. Ariadne had a power over him which was greater than that of any trainer over any animal in my knowledge, and I kept that in my mind for future meditation. When he was quiet we walked with him, still holding his horns, to the gap at the end of the field, where the handlers took him. I saw that the trees at that end concealed a heavy wooden gate and a sort of passageway made of logs.

When the bull had gone, Ariadne turned to me with genuine concern. "You did the best thing you could have done—none of us could have done better. But you must be hurt; he dragged you twice."

I almost answered that I didn't bruise easily and that she must be almost as battered as I was, but for once I had sense enough to bite my tongue.

The hostility was all gone from her eyes and she was looking at me with genuine friendliness. If she wanted to be concerned about me why not let her pamper me a little? I have noticed that helping others generally makes us like them more. So I merely smiled a little ruefully and said, "I could use a hot bath."

"That's easy enough," she replied. She clapped her hands and as servants appeared it became obvious that she was a king's daughter. Servants went off at a run to the palace to give orders for baths to be prepared and guilty-looking guards were dispatched to search the area for clues as to who had thrown the pot of coals. We walked back toward the palace and there just outside the trees was the porter with my chest. He was sitting beside it, not on it, which considering his bulk was perhaps a good thing. Ariadne ignored him after one sharp glance but I suddenly wondered if he had any connection with the thrown pot. I had assumed that if he was not an ordinary porter he was serving P'sero, but I had no real evidence for that. He fell in behind us, but at the gate of the palace my chest was taken by palace servants and he was sent away. I was not sorry to see him go.

We entered the palace past a guard whose long spears looked more ceremonial than serious, went down a long darkish corridor with some frescoes which I would have liked to see better and were suddenly in bright sunlight as we came into the central court of the great House. Even after all that had happened so far, the great court seen for the first time was a tremendous experience. On all four sides the building rose up three stories with wide balconies overlooking the court below. Over these balconies hung idlers and loungers looking at the busy scene at ground level.

In the court itself people lounged on benches around the wall, but most of the people were in motion. Men and women, servants, nobles and soldiers strolled or bustled across the court, many of them talking and laughing, or calling to friends or acquaintances. One whole side of the court at ground level seemed to be composed mostly of shrines; people went in and out of these and there seemed to be a ceremony going on in one of them. We cut across this busy scene to a broad stairway on the east side, descended a flight and after several turns passed through a room where water was being heated on portable braziers and into another room where one tub was already in place. Another was just being manhandled into the room by a crew of palace servants.

Servant girls were bringing pitchers of steaming water from the braziers and pouring the water into a giant bowl in the center of the room while other girls added cold water dipped from several enormous jars in the room. As soon as the male servants left the room Ariadne stripped off her belt and kilt and stepped into the tub that had just been brought in. Servant girls dipped water in large pitchers from the mixing bowl and came over to the tubs. The first girl poured a stream of water into the tub in front of Ariadne, who touched it with her hand murmuring a prayer in which I caught the words "living water." Ariadne touched her wet hands to breast, forehead and lips, then nodded to the girl who began to pour the water from the jar over Ariadne's body. As soon as she was finished another girl was ready with a new pitcher of water.

By this time another servant girl had poured a stream of water for me; I imitated Ariadne's gesture but did not attempt a prayer. At my nod the girl began pouring the pitcher over my back. It was almost too hot but not quite. The muscles I had bruised when the bull dragged me hurt, but it was a pleasant hurt. I found that the maids responded to slight gestures; if I bowed my head water was poured over my neck, if I stretched out an arm or a leg the stream was directed to them. As her tub began to fill from the pitchers poured over her, Ariadne half knelt, half crouched in the tub, and as it filled further leaned back and stretched out her legs so she was sitting in the tub, knees somewhat bent, leaning against the back.

Up to this point I had thought my bath the height of luxury, but when I imitated Ariadne I found that the tub was too short to straighten my legs. It was a small annoyance, but bothersome until I got the kinks out of my legs by simply sticking my feet out over the end of the tub and stretching my legs. Then I bent them again and let the girl pour more water.

When the tubs were nearly full, servant girls came in with large pieces of fine cloth which they draped over the tubs and around our necks, so that nothing could be seen of us or the tubs but our heads above the cloth. Then the girls filed out, leaving us alone. I leaned back and let the heat soak into my bones, but when I turned and saw Ariadne I began giggling.

She smiled in return and said, "I suppose it does look funny, but it keeps the heat in longer. You want a good soaking after the bruising you got."

I nodded and leaned my head back on the back of my tub which was considerably higher than Ariadne's.

"Those older tubs are comfortable," she said, "but you can't put a lid on them." When I lifted a lazy eyebrow in inquiry she continued matter-of-factly, "To be buried in, you know."

I almost sat bolt upright in the tub, but the cloth impeded my movements and I merely gave a sort of lunge. Ariadne laughed. "I suppose it sounds awful if you aren't used to it, but a bath is just as personal as clothing if you're fortunate to have your own. You wouldn't mind being buried in your best dress, would you?"

I nodded thoughtfully. "Put that way, it makes sense. But whose tub am I in now?"

Ariadne shrugged. "Oh, one of my grandmother's or great-grandmother's. This one is mine, from upstairs." Then her voice grew somber. "Chryseis, you might have needed something to be buried in today, if you hadn't been quick and clever. And the worst part of it is that I wonder if one of my Dancers was responsible."

Chapter Four: THE PRINCESS

I had been wondering why more fuss had not been made of the pot thrown in front of the bull, more questions and inquiries. But I kept silence, turning my head to look at Anadne and then resting it back again. If she were going to talk about it she would, and the relaxing heat of the bath water would be as good as wine for encouraging confidences. And if what she had to say was difficult it might be better not to look her in the face. She ducked lower in the water so she could rest her head on the back edge of her tub and closed her eyes, I saw with a quick sideways glance. Then she began to speak.

"I don't know if you know the whole story of why you Athenians were brought here for the Dance. My brother Andaroko was in Athens as the guest of your king, Aegeus. He drank too much wine and boasted of his skill with bulls—he was a famous Dancer a few years ago. Aegeus brought out his biggest and wildest bull. Andaroko tried the head leap; what I did today. He missed, and the bull killed him." There was a long pause. "Andaroko was always too sure of himself. I don't know whether Aegeus intended what happened or not. Anyway my father blamed him. He sailed himself with the fleet to the coasts of Attica. He cut off your sea traffic, even the fishermen. He sent raiding parties to destroy crops. He didn't invade and he didn't kill more Athenians than he could help. I think even then he had in mind the vengeance he wanted. When Aegeus was stubborn my father called on—Other Powers. Aegeus had to give in. My father asked for a yearly tribute of seven youths and seven maidens, all of royal or at least noble blood. Aegeus is wily though. Your companions didn't look like princes and princesses." She glanced over at me.

"You're right about Aegeus," I said slowly, thinking it out. "The people call him 'The Fox.' But I think he kept the letter of the agreement. Girls are of no great account in Athens and I think all of them came from the palace or the Hill except me. The boys—well, their fathers will be noble, some of them could even be Aegeus's sons. But their mothers will be concubines mostly—none of them will be their fathers' heirs. Unless their fathers have quarrelled with Aegeus—it would be like him to take vengeance on his enemies and satisfy your father's terms at the same time."

I looked up at the ceiling, noticing for the first time that it was elaborately painted in bright designs. "My father is a craftsman, as I told you. He's the best craftsman in Athens, not only at metal work but at every kind of making and fixing. But he'll have nothing to do with the king or the court. Other craftsmen send him things they can't make or fix, but if he knows it comes from the Hill, he refuses the work. That means he turns down almost all the work that is well rewarded. He does mending and making for poor people and asks only for what they can spare. I've seen him practically remake an old cooking pot with his own bronze and get only a jar of olives in return. That's what the poor pay with, olives and bread; it's what they live on themselves. But we've never gone hungry, and we had a good life. My father would never talk about himself but I suppose his family were noble. He brought me up not to care about such things. We live very quietly and I thought we escaped notice, but now I wonder if my being here isn't a bit of petty vengeance because my father refused to work for the king."

I didn't look at Ariadne, but her voice was warm and kind. "Thank you for telling me, Chryseis. Here in Kaphtu a craftsman as good as your father must be would take rank right after the king's children. And when I said that your companions didn't look like princes or princesses I meant just that. You did look like a princess, striding along beside P'sero." I thought she was going to say something about our strange meeting on the path and perhaps she considered it, but she lay her head back again and said, "Let me finish my story."

She went on slowly. "All of the Dancers are called children of the king. Only a few of us are children of this M'nos, but the rest are descended from my grandparents or great-grandparents. A Dancer serves three years. The first year you are a novice, learning the Dance, but if you are very good you can take part with the Dancers of that year. The year after you are a novice you are one of the Dancers of that year; seven boys and seven girls. In the third year you train novices and sometimes take part in the Dance on great festivals. The second year is your Year of Glory; what every Dancer hopes and longs for. But when M'nos came back from Athens he told us that no longer would his children dance with the bull. As soon as you Athenians can be trained you will take the place of the Dancers of the year. And because you will be taking away our Year of Glory I am not sure that one of my Dancers did not throw that pot of coals."

I looked at Ariadne compassionately. "No wonder you looked at me as if you hated me there on the field."

She smiled and shook her head. "Don't worry about me, Chryseis. I had my moments of glory as a novice. And I am Ariadne; when this M'nos dies, I and the man I will marry will rule Kaphtu. And now that I know you a little I don't begrudge you my place in the Dance. But others will. And if you or the others are killed or hurt in training…"

"I'm not sure they need worry," I said thoughtfully. "The Athenian boys, or some of them, can probably learn to do some of the leaps. But I can't imagine an Athenian girl brought up in the ordinary way doing what you and the other girls did. Because of what my father is, and my mother was, I've had quite a different life from most girls in Attica. And these are palace girls, brought up on the Hill. Some of them have probably never even seen a bull, and certainly most of them have never been allowed to run or jump or do any exercise, or work for that matter. And it's not just that." I looked into those dark eyes. "You have some sort of power over that bull. No herdsman or trainer could have calmed that beast as you did. And in the Dance he turned and moved at your will."

Ariadne returned my look steadily. "Chryseis, you are right and wrong. You and your companions will have to take our places in the Dance; M'nos has sworn it. No one has died in the Dance for many generations, but if they cannot learn the Dance M'nos will drive them out for the bull to kill. Perhaps that is even what he had in mind from the beginning. Since—certain things—happened to him he has been a bitter man." She lifted her head proudly. "Chryseis, we cannot let that happen. Not just because your companions don't deserve to die but because if they die the god will be displeased. Do you know what god the Dance serves?"

I remembered what P'sero had told me. "The sea god. The king who is called Poseidon by the Danaans."

She nodded grimly. "Posudi, we call him. The Bright King God. But Danaans and Kaphtui both have another name for him: Earthshaker. Look at the wall over there. There is a crack that has been plastered; this is an old part of the House. Two times Posudi has shaken this House down, and if we spill blood on the court of his Dance, he will shake it down again and this time it may not rise. M'nos is the priest of Posudi; I serve Ria, the Earth Mother, the Mother of the Three Kings. Her name is part of mine, and I am her Holy One. But Posudi is the ancestor of the family of M'nos and I will not let his rites be profaned." She stared ahead somberly, then began to smile. "You and I are two women together, Chryseis. Between us we will find a way to avert disaster. But for now let us get dry and dressed."

She called out and the room was full of servant
girls again. The cloths were used as towels as we
stepped out of the bathtubs. My mother's dress was
brought to me and a dress for Ariadne like the one she
had been wearing when I first saw her. We trooped
into a larger room, surrounded by servant girls and
were seated on low-backed chairs with footstools
which kept our still-bare feet off the stone floors.
Without any orders being given three-legged tables
were brought in laden with food and we were offered
our choice of wines by servant girls with flagons. I
asked for the resin-tasting wine that the farmers drink
and some was brought in after a slight delay.

Ariadne chuckled. "That jug came from the guard
room, "Chryseis. You have peasant tastes."

I nodded amiably, willing to be teased by this girl I
now felt as if I had known for years. "Peasants are
healthier than people who live in palaces. There's
nothing wrong with simple things." I helped myself to
olives and searched the plates for squid. I didn't see
anything identifiable as squid so settled for something
delicious wrapped in vine leaves. "What do you
call..." I began, then suddenly realized something.
"You've spoken to me in Kaphtui ever since we
entered the palace! How did you know..."

Ariadne shooed the maids out with a gesture and
turned to me. "I heard you talk to P'sero, there on the
hills, when I first saw you. But we will speak of that
later. First we must see what can be done about your
companions and the Dance. Things are not as bad as
they might be. We need only four who can actually
leap the bull—two boys and one other girl My Dancers

are the first in years to have eight Leapers; four will satisfy the god. You said the boys could do it and one of the girls may surprise you. The best Leapers are not always the ones you would expect."

Even in the presence of the dangers Ariadne had just revealed, my heart bounded to think of being part of the Dance I had seen a little of. Ariadne went on earnestly. "You are right in saying that the bull does my will. Part of that is training; you will catch and train your own bull. But part of it is a power some people have over animals. But, Chryseis, you have that power too; I could feel it when we were calming the bull. And if you have even a little there are ways to make it stronger. You will see."

I nodded at this; it was true enough that I was good with animals and liked them. Even the most savage shepherd dog would not bite me. Part of dealing with animals is common sense, but there is something else too; animals hate some people and like others.

Ariadne smiled at me. "Between you, P'sero and yourself have already made things better. The priestesses who went to the ship for the Thanksgiving told me that you had raised the hymn to Atane and the others sang and danced. For whatever reason you did it, that was a shrewd stroke. For my people, those who sing and dance to the gods and goddesses are priests and priestesses. Then P'sero brought you to the guest house and had you entertained, like visiting ambassadors. My father may be angry at Athens. He may have planned to treat you harshly. But he cannot treat priests and priestesses as slaves: no servant of the gods is a slave of man or woman. He cannot even treat you as captives or enemies without making P'sero look like a fool, and that would be an insult. My father will not insult P'sero; he values him and even fears him a little. The two of you have tied the hands of M'nos."

She began to chuckle. "Talk of foxes—if there is such a thing as a sea fox, P'sero is one. He is our best trader and our best captain. M'nos was not in N'sos today because no one would have believed that the ship could have come from Athens so quickly. And no ship could, except P'sero's. If he were a little younger and if I did not like and respect his wife, I would marry P'sero and make him the next M'nos."

I looked at her in surprise and she nodded with pride on her face. "Oh, yes. The husband of the daughter of M'nos is the next M'nos. We women have kept that from the days we ruled this land. Since we began trading with Egypt long ago we have taken on some of their ways. Some daughters of M'nos have married their brothers, and the son of M'nos became M'nos. But that was Ariadne's choice. The eldest daughter of M'nos is always Ariadne: the Holy Lady of the Goddess of the Land. And each Ariadne must choose the best man in Kaphtu to be her husband and the next M'nos. Then she must give him a daughter to be Ariadne again." She grinned impishly. "After that what she does is her own business: women are free in Kaphtu." A grimmer look took the place of the grin. "That freedom has not always been used wisely; I will tell you that story another time."

She rose to her feet. "Come with me, Chryseis. I am going to give orders for your companions to be brought into the house and put into the quarters set aside for the novices in the Dance. Then I want you to meet a countryman of yours; the man who taught me Danaan."

While she gave orders to servants whom she summoned by a clap of her hands, I looked around the room we had been sifting In. It was well worth looking at. The walls were crowded with designs that all somehow fit together. The lower walls were a simple wavelike design, but above that level where the walls could be rubbed against or leaned on was a frieze of enchanting dolphins, leaping and playing as I had often seen them do at sea. Two walls of the room were nothing but square pillars which supported folding doors; these were half open, giving us privacy but also air and light from a large airshaft and lightwell which was just outside the room. The braziers for the hot water had been in the area between the folding doors and the airshaft, I realized, so that the fumes from the charcoal could go up the shaft. The square openings I had seen in the roof of the House, looking at it from the hills, must have been such airshafts.

Ariadne beckoned and I followed her, while servant girls began clearing the uneaten food, chattering and helping themselves to tidbits. That was very typical of the palace of M'nos, I was to find. At any hour of the day and for most of the night you could find something to eat or drink in the palace, someone to gossip with or some other way to pass the time. The things you could not easily get, even if you were of the highest rank, were the things I had had at home without valuing them: privacy and quiet.

This last was forcibly borne on me as we went up a stair and through more rooms. As the noise grew louder I realized that all through my talk with Ariadne I had been hearing familiar noises: the noise of craftsmen at work. If the quarters we had just left were those of M'nos's family, they must have the sound of the workshop in their ears all day. As we turned into a large room with a number of men working in it, I saw familiar sights; a small goldsmith's forge near a window, a jeweler working at his bench. We passed through the large room to a door at the back, saluted by some of the workmen and ignored by others.

The door was closed, the first closed door I had seen in the House. Ariadne lifted a latch and walked in without knocking. I realized again that she was a princess and that no door in the House could be closed to her.

As I went into the room I saw a scene heart-stopping in its familiarity: a master craftsman with reddish hair sitting cross-legged on a wide bench, bent over some work in front of him, one shoulder higher than the other. But when he straightened up it was not, of course, my father's face, but the face of a stranger. "Go away, Ariadne," was his greeting. Here was one man not awed by my companion. Ariadne's statement that a master craftsman ranked with royalty was evidently not an exaggeration.

Ariadne laughed and spoke to him in Danaan. "Don't be angry, Uncle," she said. "I've brought you a compatriot. Chryseis here is the Athenian girl who will take my place in the Dance." I was standing a little behind Ariadne and on a sudden impulse I made a sign with my fingers that my father had taught me; a recognition signal for craftsmen. The master craftsman's pale eyes flickered a little but he made no other sign and he replied to Ariadne without greeting me. "I told you no Athenian could play your mad games with bulls, Ariadne. I told M'nos too, but he wouldn't listen."

Ariadne frowned at him, but not angrily: I had a sudden realization that she must get a lot of flattery and that she liked this man partly because he sparred with her. Not that she would have tolerated mere disrespect, but this man was a king in his own craft, and she could treat him as an equal. "They will do the Dance because they must, Uncle. M'nos will not be swayed. And when I said Chryseis would take my place, I meant it: she must be the tauromath. She has the Power: can you give her an amulet to strengthen it?"

The man rummaged on a shelf by his side and brought out a box. "I can give her something that will help; but if you want her to really be able to use her power you know that there's only one way. But it remains to be seen if she has any power to be strengthened." He addressed me for the first time. "Come here, child." He spilled out the box on the bench. It was filled with small seals, some of them seal rings, cut out of stone or cast in metal. "Pick up any one of these and tell me what you feel."

I picked up the nearest, a gold ring, not knowing what to expect. But I dropped it almost immediately shaking my hand and looking at the innocent-looking

object with amazement. "What did you feel?" asked
the craftsman intently.

"It was like holding a sea urchin," I said. "All
spikey."

He picked up the ring and looked at it; it had a
design of offering jars on it. "I never liked that ring,
but I didn't know why. Yes. It had better go into a
burial soon; it will do no harm in a tomb. A very strong
reaction; you do have something, child. Try this one."

I picked up a stone seal with a loop too small for a
finger; P'sero had worn one like it on a thong around
his wrist. "It feels warm," I reported. "As if my hand
were in a warm bath."

He pushed another over. "What about this?" I lay
down the stone seal reluctantly and took the new one.

"It feels greasy," I said. "No, just smoother than it
should."

He nodded. "It repels you but isn't hostile. Yes."

He turned to Ariadne. "This will take awhile," he
said. "Leave her with me; I'll bring her back to your
quarters."

Ariadne nodded and smiled at both of us. "Don't
let him browbeat you," she said to me, and to him,
"Take care of her." She turned and left the room,
leaving it somehow dimmer and quieter without her
vivid presence.

The craftsman turned his pale eyes to me, and
rubbed his long nose. "You've made a friend, girl. A
good friend to have but a dangerous one. M'nos won't
like it." He uncrossed his legs and sat on the edge of
his bench looking at me. "No need to ask whose
daughter you are. Only Lykos would have taught his

daughter the sign of Hephaestus. And you have your mother's chin. Your father may have mentioned me. We used to be good friends. I am Daedalus the Athenian."

Chapter Five: THE VEIL

The room wavered before me for a moment and I heard my father's voice as he stood on the deck of P'sero's ship in the harbor of Phaleron, my chest beside him. "If you can, seek out Daedalus the craftsman. He will help you if you need help." Then I was filled with wild excitement. This man not only knew my father, he knew my mother!

I gasped. "Yes, Daedalus, my father said to find you if I could. But please tell me what you know of my father—and my mother! I need to know!"

His voice rapped out sharply. "Put down that seal!"

I looked at my hand and found I was grasping the stone seal, the one which had felt warm. I let it go with a strange reluctance.

Daedalus looked at me between anger and amazement. "Put your compulsions on bulls, girl, not on me! By the Dog, M'nos doesn't know what he's caught in his net!" He began to laugh and put an arm around my shoulder. "Sit on the bench here with me, Chryseis. I'll tell you about your father, but I can't tell you much about your mother. For one thing I don't know much, and some of what I do know is your father's secret, not mine to tell. How long did your mother stay with you?"

I looked at him in amazement. He knew the great secret about my mother, that she had not died but had simply gone away from us, from my father and myself. I suddenly realised, despite all of her assurances and my father's, how much that still hurt. "When I was seven years old she... left."

Daedalus seemed surprised. "Eight years, counting the time she carried you. A full cycle of Aphrodite. You're fortunate, girl, as so is Lykos. She stayed with you as long as she possibly could. What's your age now?"

"Nearly fifteen," I said, goggling at him. What did he mean? What did he know? But somehow those words, "She stayed with you as long as she possibly could," made a warm glow somewhere inside me.

A thousand questions trembled on my lips, but Daedalus raised his hand. "Chryseis, I can't tell you the things you want to know about your mother. This I can tell you. You resemble her very strongly, except that your hair is darker. And you evidently have some of her power. Another cycle is ending and I'm sure that if she can see you again, she will. But that's all I can tell you."

"But... is she here in Kaphtu? Is she..."

He shook his head. "I don't know. And I can't tell you any more about her. But I can tell you about your father." I saw I would have to be content with that for now and I was eager to hear what he could tell me of my father. I fixed my eyes on his face and he grinned suddenly and rubbed his nose. "The first thing, child, is that you have a better right than Ariadne to call me 'Uncle.' Your father and I are cousins. My mother was

Merope, Pandion's sister. And Pandion was your father's father."

I gaped at him. "But Pandion…"

He nodded. "Yes. Pandion, king of Athens. Your father is Lykos, son of Pandion, brother to Aegeus the present king."

He began laughing, a dry chuckle that deepened to a deep laugh. "The gossip is already around this palace that Ariadne has made friends with a princess from Athens. For once gossip is right. Your father is not the reigning king, but he could have been if he had wanted. He was always better liked than Aegeus. But he's like me. The blood of Hephaestus runs in the family of Erechthoneus and it made craftsmen of your father and me. But your blood is just as royal, and just as divine, as Ariadne's."

My head was full of a jumble of questions. I seized one and asked it. "But why does father…"

Daedalus had a trick of knowing the question I was going to ask. "Why does he live as a poor craftsman in a city he could be king of? Because he loves his craft. Because he loves Athens. And because he wants to be near Aegina, but can't bear to live there." He gave an impatient gesture. "By the Dog, I'd love to have him here with me. But he'd never come when he could, and since M'nos quarreled with Rhadamantes…"

My head was whirling. "Who is Rhadamantes?" I interrupted in a loud voice.

Daedalus grinned at me again. "Rhadamantes is the brother of M'nos. He should be king of Ph'stos, under M'nos, of course. But he and M'nos quarreled and Rhadamantes is somewhere in Asia now. Rhadamantes and your father were good friends, better even than your father and I. Rhadamantes is another fire-head—" he touched his own rusty locks— "like your father and me. It's hard to believe he's a descendant of blue-haired Poseidon. He's red-haired and hotheaded. And your father was too close a friend of his to be welcomed by M'nos. That won't affect you, though." He smiled sourly. "M'nos will have other reasons for disliking you.

He was suddenly brisk. "Ariadne is going to wonder what happened to you. Take the stone seal I told you to drop. If you can bend my mind with it you can bend a bull's. But to be tauromath for a whole team you'll need your own seal and to get your own design you'll have to walk the Path. You'll do It. I'll back the two of you against M'nos." Still talking he led me out of the room.

I felt that he was the cleverest man, except for my father, I had ever met, and by far the most exasperating. Aegeus, P'sero, Daedalus: I was surrounded by foxes. M'nos, I was sure, would be another. So be it. I was not as innocent as I looked, myself.

Daedalus led me in the direction of the rooms Ariadne and I had bathed and eaten in, but went up a flight of stairs instead of down. We came to a room where elegantly bejeweled ladies lounged on benches; ignoring them, Daedalus crossed the room and rapped on a door. Ariadne's voice called for us to enter. We went into another richly decorated room. Ariadne stood in the center of the room once more covered by the curious veil. Daedalus looked around the room, plainly not seeing her, and raised his voice. "What are you playing at, Ariadne? Where are you?"

She spoke: "Leave Chryseis here, Daedalus. Thank you."

He didn't seem to be able to locate where her voice was coming from. He cast a sharp glance at me and then stomped out muttering in his beard, "Amulets! Vanishing tricks! M'nos doesn't know what he's started."

Ariadne looked at me. "You can see me, can't you, Chryseis? Just as you could this morning on the hill?"

I nodded slowly. "Somehow I can always see what's really there, Ariadne. It's the only way I know that I'm truly different from other people. It's not always a comfortable talent to have."

She nodded and slipped off the veil. "This is one of the treasures of our family, Chryseis, passed down from Ariadne to Ariadne, from the days when women ruled. You are the first one ever to see beyond it. It was a great shock when you met my eyes there on the hills. It could make you a dangerous enemy. But somehow we've become friends, haven't we?" She reached out her hands to me.

I took her hands and looked into her eyes. "Yes, Ariadne, we've become friends. And I want you to know that my real name, the name my mother gave me, is Britomartis. That's why I was so startled when you said that name on the field. There's some mystery about my mother, Ariadne. She—vanished—seven years ago. Daedalus knows something about her he won't tell. And he knows my father, too. Ariadne, he says my father is King Aegeus's brother."

Ariadne hugged me impulsively. "I knew you were a princess, Britomartis. Daedalus would know, we've always known he was Pandion's nephew. And if he knows something about your mother we'll get it out of him. I think that there's not much we can't do together."

I grinned at her. "Daedalus said your father doesn't even know what he's begun."

She nodded. "He's right, I think, but it doesn't do to underestimate M'nos. By now his spies will have told him everything that's happened: your arrival, the bull, our spending time together, seeing Daedalus. He's probably on his way back now; he was at Ph'stos. We need to do everything we can before he gets back."

I sketched a mock salute. "At your command, princess."

She looked serious. "I hope you are—princess—because my plan involves something you may not like. I'd like you to put on the Veil of Adis and see what your companions are doing. Do you mind that?"

I considered seriously. "No, I don't think I do. Since all this activity is partly to keep them from being killed or hurt I don't think it's unfair to listen to them without their knowledge. Does the veil work for people outside your family?"

She gave a little giggle. "It's brought a good many lovers unseen to the queen's chamber. I think it will work for you." She threw it over my head. I felt slightly cold and the room seemed a little dimmer than would be accounted for by the material of the veil before my eyes. I felt a moment of panic, then a great feeling of peace.

Ariadne reached out and touched my arm. "Remember, you can be felt, though somehow people don't seem to bump into you when you wear it. There's a slight feeling of cold when you come near it and I think people instinctively move away from it. Remember as soon as you move I have no idea where you are, but I've had enough practice wearing it so that I can give you time to get through doors and so on. Your ability to see me may be a great help sometime when I'm wearing it and you're with me. Come on."

She opened the door and stood for a moment chatting with the women in the outer chamber—ladies in waiting, I realized—while I walked through the door, through the room and out into the corridor. I kept at Ariadne's heels and of course the princess was respectfully made way for so I encountered no problems of colliding with people. But I could see that using the veil without a companion in the know could lead to problems. The corridors were busy and people who respectfully stepped aside for Ariadne would have had to be maneuvered around if I had been alone. As we passed a lightwell from which bright sunlight spilled into the corridor I saw I cast no shadow. The sunlight reminded me that it was still only early afternoon; I seemed to have lived years since waking this morning on P'sero's ship.

Ariadne paused outside a door; lounging near it was a guard with a familiar face—one of the guards who had been with us on the ship. He saluted Ariadne respectfully.

"How are the Athenians settling in?" she asked.

"It's hard to tell, my Lady," he replied. "The clever one went off with one of your ladies this morning and hasn't returned and the rest only speak their own language."

I could sense the amusement Ariadne was trying to keep out of her voice. "The clever one?" she asked.

"Yes, my Lady," he replied. "One of them is a girl with brown hair and a big chin. She was never seasick at all and she was all over the ship asking questions and poking into things. By the time the voyage was half over she could speak our language pretty well."

The guard smiled reminiscently. "She was curious about everything. I showed her how we catch the little squid in our village and she fixed the loose handle on my knife; she said her father is a craftsman. If she were here, Lady, I could ask her about the others; she was friendly with everyone. But the rest just stare at you even if you try to say something in their language." Ariadne nodded. "You must tell me more about the clever one." I knew she was teasing me and considered moving closer and giving her a good pinch. But she went on. "But right now make an excuse to go into the room. Come back and tell me what they're doing. Here." She stopped a servant girl who was carrying a basket of fruit down the corridor and took the basket from her. "Take this in to them."

The guard saluted and took the basket, leaving his long spear against the wall. I kept close on his heels as he opened the door and went in. The Athenians had been talking but as soon as the guard came in they stopped. They made no acknowledgment of the fruit, and when he gave them the common Kaphtui greeting,

"Blessings," they stared at him uncomprehendingly. It was the first word I had learned.

The guard shrugged and went out, closing the door. I realized it would have to be opened before I could go out, if I were not to give my presence away. Invisibility had its complications. When they were sure the guard was gone, Euphoros burst out, "He didn't even have his spear. We could have grabbed him and taken his knife and sword and gotten out of here."

Glaukos replied in a patient tone, this was evidently a running argument between them. "And where would we go? Even if we got out of this place we don't speak their language and we don't look like them. We'd be rounded up again in no time. If Chryseis were here at least she could talk to them for us, but we don't know what they've done to her. You may not like her, but she's one of us. and I'm not doing anything until we find out what's happened to her." My heart warmed to Glaukos.

One of the girls spoke up. It was Alceme, a minx who gave herself airs because her hair was as golden as mine used to be. She had been the most malicious of the girls when we were on the ship.

"Don't worry about *her*," she sneered. "She's with her *friends*. But I'm not taking part in any mad escape attempts. We can't swim back to Athens and if we could old Aegeus would send us right back; we're his blood-price for the Cretan prince. Chryseis was no fool—if we want to survive here we've got to get along with these people. They're friendly enough if you boys aren't snarling at them."

Despite her malice toward me I liked Alceme better after that speech. She wasn't afraid to stand up to the boys, and she showed some sense, even if, as I suspected, her willingness to "get along with these people" was based on a calculation that her attractions would win her special favors, whatever happened to the others.

But Euphoros was maddened by this opposition from a female. He began to shout. "I tell you I won't be enslaved or sacrificed to their bull god. My father is a great noble. We should die proudly trying to escape rather than let them slaughter us or treat us as slaves."

Except for Glaukos the other boys seemed to be carried along by his words. I admired their courage but not their intelligence. Glaukos and Alceme had been quite right. But any moment they might do something foolish and throw away the good work P'sero and I had done.

I lost my temper. "Fools!" I shouted. "You won't be enslaved or killed. If you show courage and good sense you can have great honor." I hadn't realized the effectiveness of a voice seemingly coming out of empty air. Either something about the veil itself or simply the effect of not having a visible figure to focus on confused them about the direction of my voice and after frantically looking around most of them looked up into the air above their heads. Euphoros's mouth was gaping open. Alceme's drawn-back lips revealed clenched teeth and even Glaukos had paled. I noticed that the pallor brought his freckles into relief. One girl screamed and another gave a sob. One of the boys,

Menesthius, who I remembered was a priest's son, exclaimed, "It is the goddess!"

I had spoken completely out of impulse, but at Menesthius's words a plan sprang into my head. I spoke again, trying to make my voice big and impressive, though I think now that the veil did something to voices too. "You are here to take the place of the Cretan prince in a great Dance for King Poseidon" I nearly said "Kaphtui prince" but remembered in time to use the name the Danaans used. "This dance has always been danced by the children of King M'nos and if you do it well you will be honored and richly rewarded." I had learned from P'sero that Dancers were given presents by M'nos and his court and I thought that this bit would appeal to Alceme. I had to reassure them all too. "There is danger in the Dance but if you are faithful and courageous I will protect you. The girl Chryseis will be set over you as your leader. Obey her in all things and you will be fortunate. Disobey her and I will remove my protection from you. Rememher what I have told you!"

I stopped speaking and moved over to the door to keep out of the way and wait for an opportunity to leave. A number of things I should have said crowded into my mind, but I bit my tongue. If I talked too long someone might recognize my voice or have inconvenient doubts.

When it became clear that the voice they had heard was through speaking, the Athenians looked at each other with fear and wonder in their eyes. Menesthius was the first to speak. "It can only have been Athena, protectress of our city. She heard the hymn we sang to her on the ship. And Chryseis raised that hymn. I will hear no more speaking against her."

I could have hugged him; It was just the effect I had wanted to produce. Euphoros was sweating and trembling; if there was courage behind his bluster it was for physical danger, not for this kind of thing. Alceme's eyes were calculating, but I could tell she was impressed.

Glaukos was the first to smile. "You heard the goddess, friends, we are under her protection! We need have no fear. And Chryseis is safe."

I frowned at this under my veil of invisibility. I wanted Glaukos as an ally, but this was no time for anything warmer.

Menesthius stepped forward. "Let us sing the hymn to Athena again, friends, to give her thanks." For the first time a qualm shot through me. Pretending to be a goddess is said to be a risky business; there are grisly stories even about Athena, stories of the vengeance of the gods on mortals who challenged their prerogatives.

I remembered my father's voice saying, "The Olympians did not make the world and they do not rule it. But they can do great good or great harm to mortals. You need not worship them, but do not offend them. The gods are bad enemies."

I had never been afraid of Athena, though, I thought as her hymn rang in my ears. The old statue in the ancient square temple in the Acropolis looked like nothing human, but on smaller statues and engravings I had seen she had the same rounded but determined chin I had inherited from my mother. I suppose that when my mother left us when I was seven I even imagined Athena as a substitute mother and I haunted her temple for awhile. That was when the priestess had warned me out of the private precincts. I grinned. remembering the guard's reference to my "big chin." The Kaphtui admire small pointed chins and big dark eyes.

Just then the door opened and the guard looked in. I suppose they could hear the hymn outside the door and Ariadne would have been waiting for a chance to give me an opportunity to slip out again. But the irritating man stood blocking the door, with his hand on the latch while they finished the hymn. Then he asked in slow, accented Danaan, "What you do?"

Glaukos turned to him with dignity and said, "Our goddess has given us a message."

The guard shook his head in puzzlement and turned to Ariadne who was keeping out of sight in the corridor. I just managed to slip past him as the turn of his body gave me space, and I touched Ariadne's arm to let her know I was out. She gestured to him to shut the door.

He asked, "Did you hear, Lady? I think they said something about their goddess."

Ariadne nodded. "They said she had spoken to them. It is likely enough. Atane is fond of the people of that city and the blood guilt for my brother falls on their king, not on these children. Presently I will send the 'clever one' back to them and you can speak to them through her. Treat them with respect, all of you guards. They will be Dancers as soon as they can be trained." She turned and we threaded our way back through the corridors to her room. When we were inside she put the pin through the door latch and turned to me as I took off the veil.

"I've never seen anyone else use the veil," she said. "It looks strange to see you appear from the feet up as you draw it off. I see that you did more than listen to them, 'goddess.'" She smiled a little grimly. "I didn't say I was Athena, but of course they thought so," I replied. "The boys were working themselves up to attack the guard, and I had to do something." I told her what I had said, repeating the words as exactly as I could remember them and she nodded thoughtfully.

"That was well done," she said. "They will obey you now. I am going to try to train your group as much like ordinary novices in the Dance as possible. I don't think M'nos will interfere. You will be leader of the novices; when M'nos forces this year's Dancers to step aside you will become Mistress of the Dance. But I will try to delay the change until you can be properly trained; if some of you appear as novices with this year's Dancers perhaps M'nos will be satisfied. I would like to keep you with me, Britomartis, but if you are to lead them you must live with them."

I nodded agreement. "Without me to interpret they'd be impossible to train. I'll have to start them learning the language. Send for me when you can. I don't want to lose you as a friend. But probably many people will be jealous if we spend too much time together."

Her head lifted proudly. "I am Ariadne. I do not set aside my friends for a few gossiping tongues. But you are right, my 'clever one,' there will be jealousy. Even my friendship with Daedalus causes tongues to wag.

The gossip already says you are a princess. Act like one and you will be treated like one, and that will make our friendship easier. Even where people can hear call me Ariadne and not lady or princess. But we had better not use your true name in public; the priestesses will not like it if a mortal has a goddess's name."

She smiled suddenly. "Ka-ria-se," she said. "In the old language we still use for sacred things that would be 'Beautiful queen of the land,' just as 'Ka-ria-tu' is beautiful island land and 'Kaphtu' is 'Beautiful golden island.' Say your name so when you talk to my people instead of running it all together; priestesses and royalty have the old names, and it will add to your prestige. We are playing a dangerous game, Britomartis, and we will have to be clever about even little things. Your words to your compatriots were a promise; we must make that promise good."

There seemed nothing more to say, and we held each other's hands for a moment. Then with that proud lift of her head she unlatched the door and we went out of the room together.

Chapter Six: THE PATH

Ten days later I was sitting in what was already my accustomed place on the corner of Daedalus's bench, swinging my legs and arguing with Daedalus, who insisted that I call him Uncle, as Ariadne did. I was barefoot and dressed only in my kilt, which I wore everywhere. Since a girl in a kilt could only be a Dancer this dress was an instant passport to any part of the palace. I was becoming known as myself in some parts of the palace, but thousands of people live in the House and most of them had never heard of me, or for that matter of Athens. But for anyone in the House it was enough that I was a Dancer; in N'sos a Dancer has the honor Athenians give to a warrior, a priest or an entertainer, all put into one.

For of course the Dance itself at the great festivals and the constant practice for the Dance are entertainment as well as worship of the god. Once you have taken part in the Dance itself you are known as an individual all over N'sos, especially if you are a Leaper. But even the novices are watched and their talents assessed. Anyone who can get away from his or her duties will watch the Dancers practice, and if they cannot see the Dancers they will settle for the novices.

The early novice practice, of course, is not with the bull. Much of it is running and jumping and tumbling on the ground, but soon you begin to practice with a figure of a bull made of wood. Daedalus had in his workshop a marble figure from the Circle Islands, of a harper. At first when you looked at it, it seemed laughable, like the figure a child makes playing with clay; arms like tubes and a little bump of a nose. But as you looked at it longer it seemed the pure essence of a harper caught in streams of white light, so that a real harper seemed bumpy and dark and contorted compared to it. The practice bull was like that. It had originally been, I suppose, a twisted root of some tremendous old tree that looked a little like a bull. Some skillful craftsman long dead had carved it just enough and set the horns of a real bull in the oblong lump which was the head. And now it was more a bull than a real bull; all the strength and pride and menace of the bull embodied in its blocky shape.

Its back was scored with crosswise lines to give purchase, and we did countless vaults and handsprings across that back. It could sit on a low platform with wheels which pulled with ropes to set it in motion but I never trusted that as practice for vaulting a running bull; a real bull runs with its legs and moves up and down. Nor is the motion you make to dodge a cart on wheels the right motion to dodge a real bull if you miss a leap. I suppose these were partly excuses, for I didn't like to see the image put on its cart. Pulled on wheels it seemed to lose the danger and majesty it had when planted on the ground on the four twisted roots that were its legs.

Ariadne left as much of our training as she could to the last year's Dancers, who by tradition were the Trainers of the novices. It was the chief Trainer, another girl called T'ne who usually drilled me. I learned that T'ne was not a name, but a nickname. It meant Wise Lady and usually meant a healer or a priestess. It had the same sounds that went into A-ta-ne the Kaphtui name for Athena. Our T'ne was neither a healer nor outside the Dance, a priestess; but she was wise in bulls. She had been the tauromath of her year, the Dancer who by some strange sympathy with animals and the aid of an amulet of power controls the bull and makes him run and toss as required by the dance.

She and I worked with Winey, which was the nickname of the great red-brown bull used by the Dancers of this year. One thing had prevented M'nos from throwing us Athenians into the Dance immediately was the unbending tradition of the Dance, which said that the Dancers of each year must catch their own bull. But T'ne and I both feared that M'nos might keep the letter of his oath by withdrawing Ariadne and Ph'dare, her sister, from the Dance; Ariadne was the tauromath and Ph'dare had the power, though she had never trained it.

T'ne became a good friend; she was a tall silent girl, thin and even bony but very graceful when she moved. Her real name was N'dare, "Child conceived by the goddess." The Trainers did not have the same reason as the Dancers to dislike us, of course, we were not a threat to their Year of Glory, which was past. But T'ne could have resented us as supplanters of her own people. Because she did not and because the others of her year were used to fellowing her lead, she made things much easier for us Athenians.

By experimenting she and I found that using the seal Daedalus had given me I could control the bull for myself or for one other Dancer, and up to half the length of the field. But I could not control him as well as I needed to be tauromath. It was over that that Daedalus and I were quarreling. He was maintaining that he could not give me a seal with more power unless he made one for me based on a vision, which I could only have if Ariadne would send me along the Path. "It's no use her trying to protect you," he said. "You're the first real friend she's had and she's afraid you may come to harm on the Path. But you'll come to more harm if a bull breaks loose from your mind and tramples you."

I had no fear for myself, especially from Winey who was well broken in to the routine of the Dance. He would even change pace to avoid trampling a Dancer who was clumsy on the Roll Under, and a bull has no natural instinct not to trample a man, though they claim a horse has. Winey would not hurt me, I knew, but harm could come to my companions if I could not control him.

I had grown to love all of them except perhaps Euphoros and one or two of the more sniveling girls, who made a song and dance each time they had to practice in the kilt. Certainly I loved my other three Leapers: Alceme, Glaukos and Menesthius. Alceme was the most unexpected of my new friends but I had soon learned that her spite on the ship had been based on jealousy. She could not stand not to be the center of male attention and with my language learning I had monopolized every male on the ship. She had more muscle than appeared under that silky skin and as soon as she learned how Dancers were admired she was mad to be a Leaper. She was the only Athenian girl except myself who took to wearing the kilt regularly, and with her golden hair and well developed figure she looked spectacular in it. She became a good Leaper too, cool-headed and with that little touch of cool self-interest that marks the survivor of any dangerous game. She would never throw her life away, but she would risk it on a fighting chance.

Glaukos was cool, steady and utterly dependable; he would gladly have given his life for me, which made him a responsibility. His devotion was never obtrusive but it was bothersome nevertheless. Menesthius was the most intelligent of the boys, deft and clever and with a heart-warming vein of dry humor. I placated Euphoros by making him the chief of those who danced but did not leap; by tradition if the leader of the Leapers is one sex the leader of the "ground dancers" is the other, and none of the other four boys had any great advantage over Euphoros. I can hardly remember the faces of some of the quieter ground dancers, though I was fond of them at the time; they were my little flock. But those who are Leapers together are bound by a bond that is never forgotten.

So I knew that though I argued with Daedalus, he was right. I needed the greater power a seal made from my vision would give me.

"All right," I said. "I'll talk to Ariadne. Now what about M'nos? When will he return from Ph'stos?"

Daedalus replied patiently, "As I have told you, he is not at Ph'stos but at the House of the Three Kings near Ph'stos. That House is a summer palace and very pleasant. Rhadamantes built it for his bride. There is nothing to cause remark about M'nos staying there. But so long as he is there his options are open. He can come back and denounce everything that has been done, because it was done while he was away. He can come back with some sudden stroke of policy. Or he can stay there and let us stew, which he seems to be doing. When you and P'sero and Ariadne took things into your own hands you put M'nos into a dilemma. When he solves that dilemma to his advantage he will return. Meantime his spies are everywhere; assume he knows all that happens."

I sighed and got up: we had been over this ground before. It was time for my next stop; my evening visit to Ariadne. Our team ate together in our quarters, two sleeping rooms with a large common room in between, somewhat earlier than Ariadne ate with her ladies. We trained in the morning, took a little food and a siesta during the heat of the day, then trained until the evening meal. There was a common bathtub for the girls and one for the boys; the evening social life centered around a series of baths while sore muscles were massaged and Kaphtui hair styles experimented with. I exercised my prerogative as leader of the novices to take first bath and then visit my growing circle of Kaphtui friends. There was little mingling between girls and boys except on the practice field and the evening conversation of Athenian girls bored me. Alceme occasionally came with me on my visits. Ariadne was cool to her; she wanted me to herself. But Daedalus treated her with ironic gallantry and I saw Alceme's calculating eyes rest on him sometimes. Daedalus was wealthy and powerful and Alceme always thought several moves ahead. It was part of what made her a good Dancer.

Yesterday evening Alceme and I with Glaukos and Menesthius had gone down to dinner at Amnisos with P'sero and his family. Or rather Alceme and I had eaten with P'sero's wife, Riamare, and his daughter M'pha while Glaukos and Menesthius had eaten with P'sero and N'suto, though afterward we had all gathered by the fire. Alceme's stock of Kaphtui words were growing rapidly and she tried a little stilted conversation with M'pha while Riamare and I measured each other. After a sharp glance at P'sero and myself when we arrived to make sure she had nothing to worry about as a wife, Riamare was friendly but a little cool. I tried no tricks with her, simply let her see that I loved P'sero as a father and was prepared to love her for his sake. She was not someone who would give her friendship lightly but I could see that if she trusted you she would be a friend worth having.

She was a small dark woman. Ariadne had told me that she was always a little afraid of Riamare, who could be fierce when aroused. She came of the oldest stock in the land, Ariadne said, the small dark people who were here when the sea god in the form of a bull brought Aropa to these shores to be the mother of future kings.

Riamare was skeptical of that story. "It is true enough," she said, "that the house of M'nos are children of blue-haired Posudi. But kingship came to this land with the tall long-headed men like my husband who love the sea and know ships. Men of that stock came here in their ships and married the women of my stock just as the sons of Posudi married the daughters of Kariatu, the nymph of this island. The god was too strong for our goddesses, after all he is the son of Ria. So men took over the rule. But Ariadne chooses her husband, who is the next M'nos and the gods and goddesses have equal honor. Have you heard my husband say, 'The axe has two blades'?"

"Yes," I said, remembering the Hall of Partridges and his words with T'ne.

"That is the strongest saying on Kaphtu," she said. "It means that for each god there is a goddess, and both are equally honored. The double axe of the Earth, L'aburia, is the symbol of our land and people. The two blades mean god and goddess, man and woman. It is called D'aboria, the gods' double axe, or L'aburia, the ship axe, or L'aburias, the ship axe of the rulers, to distinguish it from the common ship axe for hewing timbers. But always the two blades are equal, and the male and female sides of things are equal. This is the only land where that is so."

She paused thoughtfully. "The House of Knossos is called Aburiantos, the House of the double Earth axe. But M'nos has always tried to claim that House and that axe for his own, to call it L'aburiasu, the ship axe of the king, and L'aburiantos, the house of the ship axe. What he does not know is that if he succeeds he will spoil the balance that makes this land. The goddesses will share equally with the gods, but they will not let the gods have the upper hand. If the balance is destroyed, they will let the House fall, and the house of M'nos fall. Posudi will pull it down himself, for his temper is easily aroused if he is not restrained by the goddesses."

As she talked on in her deep, strong voice I thought that she was the strangest woman I had met on Kaphtu and perhaps the wisest. I wondered if when she talked of gods and goddesses it was a way of talking of men and women and meant that if men tried to get the upper hand the women would revolt. In most lands that would be a threat to laugh at, but the women of Kaphtu have great power. As I walked home with the others under the stars I saw that my and Ariadne battle with M'nos was part of a greater battle between men and women, and that if the men won they would be the greatest losers. Except for my mother all the Danaan women I had known seemed only half alive compared to these powerful Kaphtui women.

All this was in my mind when I argued with Ariadne the evening after my talk with Riamare. "You talk of the dangers of the Path, Ariadne, but the dangers of not taking the Path are worse. Nothing is more likely than that M'nos will take you out of the Dance and put me in your place. As it is now I cannot control Winey well enough for a Dance, and that blood you talked about will be spilled on the court of the Dance. If that happens all of our plans are worthless." She lifted her hand in surrender. "All right, Britomartis, you win. But I've had a bad feeling about the Path ever since the new priestess took the place of the old one. She calls on Akata with her mouth but her heart calls on Ekota or even Ukota."

Of course, all the names of the Gods Below are euphemisms. The god that the Danaans call Hades the Kaphtui call Adis—A-di-su—Holy god-king. But he is also E-di-su the Dark god-king and U-di-su the god-king of the Dead. In the same way Akato, the Holy beautiful wise one, is also Ekota the One wise in dark power, and Ukota the One wise in the power of death. But to call on any of Those Below by their "unlucky" names is deliberately to call on their darker and deadlier sides.

The Kaphtui claim to have taught the Danaans the true names and natures of the gods, but my father says that before the Danaans came to the shores of the Sea our religion was simpler and purer. "We called on Zeus as Diwa, the sky god," he used to say, "and the women called on Ria the Mother and perhaps Hestia of the Hearth. Except for the Days of the Dead only evil men disturbed Hades or Hecate. Since we knew nothing of the sea we had no need to know of King Poseidon except as Hippos, the horse god."

Ariadne was respectful of my father's sayings, but did not always agree with them. "What do men know?" she said. "Perhaps your fathers could call only on the sky god but your mothers will have called on the other two Queens as well. Hera for births and marriages and Ida for the crops. Even horse herders' wives must grow gardens. And it is not well to offend the three Young Queens either, or the Three Young Lords. They say in the Mysteries…" Here she shot me

73

a sharp glance and made a sign with her fingers. Luckily I had learned the countersign from my mother. "They say in the Mysteries," she went on in a lower voice, "that there is a Great One over all the gods. It would make sense only to worship that One. But to honor one of those from Oriaposu and not the others is foolish. They are all jealous of each other."

I remembered my father saying, "It is the young gods and goddesses that cause all the trouble." There was some kind of joke about that between him and my mother that I did not understand. But now Ariadne went on in a serious tone. "Britomartis, there is a story about my family I have not told you. After my brother and I were born my father quarreled with my mother, P'sephae. After they had separated a child was born to her. She swore a god had come to her in the form of a great white bull. I remember my nurse saying, 'Any god can seem to be a bull, but not everything that seems to be a bull is a god.' My half brother was called Astariano—Holy wise king of the land—but he was a strange child. He used to frighten other children, and the priestesses hinted his father had been one of Those Below. Not long after my brother Andaroko died he walked the Path to see what the gods wished of him. He never returned." She shuddered. "They say he still walks the Path—sometimes as a man, sometimes as a bull, sometimes as a mixture of both. No good sign has come to any who have walked the path since and some... some have not returned." She looked at me.

I looked back at her steadily. 'That is not good to hear, Ariadne. But like it or not I must walk the Path."

I was thinking of these words the next evening as I stood in one of the rooms off the main court, dressed in one of the short jackets that made me conscious of my exposed breasts as my kilt never did, and a ridiculously clumsy sheepskin skirt, Kaphtui ceremonial wear. In sacred things people change slowly. The sheepskin skirt may have gone back to days when the women and men of Kaphtui wore only the skins of animals and did not know how to weave cloth.

I stood in a small anteroom off the court; before me was a sunken area with steps going down into it, not unlike the areas in which bathtubs were placed in some parts of the House. Beyond me was a slightly larger room open to the one I stood in except for a low wall surmounted by three pillars. Around three sides of the larger room were benches, and the benches were filled with priestesses. Ariadne, pale but determined, sat at the right hand of the priestess of Akata, who now rose and came over to me.

"When the mist arises, go down the steps," she said. "As you go deeper in turn always to the left." Her eyes were like the eyes of a serpent, and I looked away from her. 'To the left." she repeated. She tied a cord around my wrist and went back to her bench paying it out; it was supposedly my lifeline to the everyday world.

I looked at the pit in front of me. An ordinary rectangular pit in the floor, lined with stone. On its floor was spread fine white sand which would show the slightest footprint. If the spell worked I would never touch that floor; the sand was to reveal any attempted deception. Now the priestess was back in her place and the chant began, a low moaning, droning chant endlessly repeated. My skin prickled, as it had at the gold ring in Daedalus's workshop.

As the chant continued gray wisps of fog or smoke began to arise from the floor of the pit. Presently the entire pit was obscured by waving streamers that reminded me of Ariadne's Veil of Adis. Somehow the memory gave me courage and I started down the steps. The fog grew thicker and thicker and seemed to form a tunnel or corridor. I went along it until I came to a branch. To the left the darkness hovered but to the right there seemed to be a hint of golden light. I hesitated, then made up my mind. Weighing the snake-like eyes of the priestess against the promise of that golden light, the light easily won. I went right.

Somewhere in the far distance there was a sound like a bull bellowing, but it grew fainter as I turned to the right again and then again, following the light. If I were walking in the room I had started out in I would be walking in larger and larger circles; by now I would have run into a wall. The light was growing strange and the ground became uneven under my feet. As I climbed up a gentle slope the fog thinned and vanished. It had been evening when I started my walk but overhead a bright sun blazed. I was standing on the edge of a gentle depression on a low green hill. Around me were other hills, a valley and a river. But of the great House there was no sign at all.

Chapter Seven: THE GRYPHON

I felt a sense of great lightness and peace. It was like waking from one of those dreams where you have grasped the secret of the universe and for a moment you feel you still know it. A voice seemed to have just stopped singing and far away in the air some flying creature that glistened in the sunlight was just going beyond the range of sight. When I glanced down at my wrist and saw that the cord had gone it didn't seem to matter at all. I walked up the slope of the hill and looked around me. Surely those were the hills across the Kariatos which I had descended with P'sero. This place was exactly like the valley in which N'sos stood except that it was completely bare of human habitation. The hill which had been carved and covered with the great house was as it must have been countless centuries ago, uncarved, unbuilt on, with grass and flowers growing on its breast. I wandered on over the crest of the hill and my wandering steps led me to a little hollow on its other side.

Lying there in the hollow was a creature out of a dream or a vision. It had an eagle's head but with great feathered ears, sloping now over its head. There was something like a crown on the top of its head, looking as if it grew there. The forelegs were feathered but much more massive than a bird's legs though they ended in great claws. The body and the great hind legs were those of a lion. It was curled in a circle like a sleeping dog, its great beak near its hind legs, its tail curved around its body and its wings half covering it. It was profoundly asleep, and there was a hint of exhaustion in the abandon of the sprawled limbs. And crawling silently straight for its head was a wickedly fanged serpent with some sort of bulge near the head. In a moment the serpent would strike.

Though I remembered every detail of that scene I have never been able to remember the words of warning I cried out. Their effect was explosive. The tremendous bulk of the creature was propelled into the air by one convulsive jerk of its mighty hind legs. The mighty wings beat once, twice, three times to keep the creature in the air. A gryphon! It was a gryphon! I remembered an ivory carving I had seen from the north.

The serpent had moved quickly but not quickly enough. After the lunge that just missed the leaping gryphon it reared its body up. From the bulge near its head sprouted stubby wings which seemed to help raise the head as they beat frantically. But the creature never had a chance. The gryphon's wings folded, the eagle head darted out, the mighty beak snapped behind the serpent's head. The two creatures came back to earth, but the serpent was broken while the gryphon landed lightly on claws and paws, the dead serpent dangling from its mouth.

It dropped the serpent immediately and began wiping its beak on the ground. Nothing could have conveyed more clearly the deadly poison its assailant had carried. Stepping around the carcass I loosed the absurd sheepskin skirt and used it to wipe the gryphon's beak clean of the black blood. Somehow I was not surprised when a clear, cold voice issued from that beak as I finished my task. "Cast the creature and your skirt into the crack in the ground yonder. Do not touch it."

Casting around for two sticks I lifted the serpent's heavy body on them and half carried, half dragged it to the hole. The sticks and my skirt followed it down. Acrid fumes came from the crack and I wondered if the serpent had come out of it. I walked back to the gryphon, which was lying on the ground on its belly, its head erect, its front legs extended before it, its hind legs up at its sides; the pose of a carved sphinx. The great head even in that position, was higher than mine. Its colors ranged from dark gold on its body to bronze color on its feathers, but the eyes with which it fixed me by dipping its beak were pale gold with black irises shaped like narrow pointed leaves.

"Why did you cry out?' the high, remote voice asked. The beak moved only slightly; I wondered if there were softer parts inside to form the words or if the voice was only in my mind.

"It was creeping up on you!" I replied. "You were asleep! It wasn't fair!"

The voice went on inexorably. "Suppose I had been stalking it? Would you have warned it, then?"

I tried to answer honestly. "I don't know. It looked evil. And you're so beautiful."

The voice spoke again. "Can you tell good and evil by looks, then?"

I looked into its eyes. "I think you can, if you look deep enough and long enough. Evil can appear beautiful for awhile, but it always gives itself away." I remembered the look of viciousness that had distorted the lovely face of a court lady when my father refused her work.

The gryphon nodded almost indifferently. "You may ask me three questions," it said.

I almost laughed out loud. A fabulous monster which played question games by rules! I had answered three questions, now it would answer three. What did I most need to know? I decided to begin diplomatically. I looked at the crownlike protrusion on its brow. "Are you the king of the gryphons?" I asked.

The massive head nodded. "I am Gyros the Lord of the Gryphon tribe. All winged things respect my name save only the winged serpents like the one I slew at your warning."

I was beginning to gather my wits. "What is this place?' I asked next.

"It is a world different from yours but very near it," the gryphon replied. "Some call it Oriaposu, the throne land of the bright king." I realized he was speaking Kaphtui but an older form than I was used to. I thought he had finished, but he added, 'Those you call gods live in this land, as well as others."

One question left. I wracked my brain but then let my heart decide. "I am Britomartis, daughter of Britomartis, called Chryseis. My mother is like me in face but her hair is brighter. Is she in this land?" I waited, my breath caught.

"I cannot answer that question," came the clear remote voice, "but you will learn the answer for yourself. Because I cannot answer it, I owe you an answer, and I will answer presently the question you should have asked, which is how to return to your own place, where you are needed. Also I owe you three favors; for your shout, for wiping my beak and for disposing of the serpent. Come to my shoulder."

I walked over to the massive shoulder.

"Reach your hand into my neck feathers," said the creature. "Past the outer feathers, near the skin. Pull out one of the little feather there." The great feathers on the surface were like bronze saws but the feathers inside were soft and the skin was warm. My hand came out holding a beautiful little feather of pure gold which curled around my fingers. "Keep it close to your skin," said the gryphon. "If you need me, cast it from you and I will come to your aid. Twice it will return to you, the third time it will return to me. You had better not wait too long now; time behaves strangely between this land and yours. Climb on my back unless you wish to be carried."

I thrust the feather into my hair, close to the skin. Then I grasped the stiff feather, got my foot on the root of a wing and swung astride his neck. Hardly was I settled when he gave a mighty spring and the great wings beat the air again. We soared above the hill and glided down to the sea. I recognized the bay on which Amnisos stood, but empty of every sign of human habitation. The gryphon landed at the foot of a cliff which was pierced with a great cave. I slipped off the gryphon's neck.

I recognized the Holy Cave which gave Amnisos its initial "A." It was a place women went for help in childbirth. P'sero had told me of it and pointed it out on our visit to his house.

"In the cave is a pillar. Walk around it keeping always to the left, since you are going from a high world to a low one. You will soon find yourself at home. Hurry back to where your friend waits for you."

Then for the last time there was that mighty spring and the beat of wings. Faster than I would have thought possible he dwindled into the sky. I looked around me almost resentfully. I had seen nothing of this world, which seemed to hold some great promise for me. The sun was no ordinary sun; as it beat on me I felt more alive, more powerful than I had ever felt. But the gryphon's last words suggested that Ariadne needed me. I shrugged and took a pretty pebble from the beach, tucking it next to my skin under the belt of my kilt, which I had worn under my sheepskin skirt. Then I walked into the cave.

Feeling foolish I walked around the pillar, keeping always left. If left was "down," where would I have ended if I had followed the priestess's advice? The shapes of the cave seemed to alter slightly as I walked and the light seemed to fade rapidly. Presently I glanced at the mouth of the cave and saw stars. I walked out of the cave and saw the city of Amnisos, holy place of the fruit of the sea, sleeping on the shore. It felt late, and no one stirred on the streets.

I began to run toward the road to N'sos. I felt light and strong, as if I could run forever. There seemed to be a light around me which made it impossible to stumble on the twisting streets. It was like running in a dream, with no sense of fatigue and almost no sense of time. I passed the rock where Ariadne had stood, but that was almost the only thing that caught my attention on that strange run.

Suddenly the House loomed before me. I turned off the causeway and went to the south entrance, where I knew the guard was easiest to evade. The corridor was dark but I seemed to be able to see the frescoes better than I had ever seen them—a stiff archaic procession of tribute bearers probably often repainted. The guard room cast a yellow light on the corridor from several lamps left burning. If anyone was looking out they could not help seeing me, but I knew the guards who were awake would be playing some game. I slipped past like a ghost, suddenly realizing that my feet had been bare all this time. I had not felt the stone road and my feet were not cold.

Now I was in the Great Court, which was silent and empty for once, though there were lights in some windows above. I went toward the room I had entered in my sheepskin skirt that evening, how could it be so late? There was a guard at the door, but he was asleep on his feet, leaning on his spear. I slipped past, feeling as if I had on the Veil of Adis.

In the room there was light from a dozen lamps but all the priestesses were asleep, sprawled on each other's shoulders. The priestess with serpent's eyes was snoring slightly, slouched on her left-hand neighbor. Ariadne slept alone, crumpled into a pathetic ball, her neighbors respecting her royalty even in sleep.

As I came into the room snake-eyes opened her eyes and gave me a surprised and malevolent glare. She struggled to straighten up, waking Ariadne in the process. Ariadne leapt to her feet and flew straight to my arms. "Oh Britomartis," she cried, "you came back!"

I hoped her use of my name would pass as a prayer to the goddess whose temple my mother had served.

The priestess's voice came harsh from behind her. "Do not thank the maiden, Lady, but thank Akata, whose mercy returned your friend. If we had not kept up our chant..." She paused, not sure how big a lie to tell.

I ignored her and pulled Ariadne toward the door. "Come on," I said. "We both need our beds; training tomorrow."

The priestess interrupted. "Wait. I must know your vision." I looked at her and she faltered. "The symbol at least," she said, "for my goddess."

I shrugged. "A great golden gryphon," I said, "killing a winged snake." I looked at her hard as I said "snake."

"A lie," she caterwauled. "There are no gryphons where I sent you."

I snapped back, "Perhaps I didn't go where you sent me." Then I pulled the sleepy Ariadne out the door, half carried her to her rooms and handed her over to her ladies who were taking turns waiting up for her; an edifying contrast to the sleeping priestesses. She was emotionally drained and if we had started talking we would have gone on all night.

The next morning I arose at the first light and stole out of the sleeping room. I found at training time that the other girls had not known I had come back. I felt light-hearted and rested. For once I presumed on my "niece" relationship with Daedalus: I had the apprentice who slept in his antechamber rout him out of bed, gave him the pebble I had picked up on the shore outside the cave and told him how I wanted It carved. I arrived at Ariadne's room at the same time as her breakfast and we shared bread, fruit and steaming herb tea sweetened with honey while I told her my story.

"And the sun was high in the sky?" she asked again. "Britomartis, it must he the Bright Land, the land of the gods, that you went to. There are traditions in our family; the first M'nos is supposed to have visited the Kings there and received laws for our land. The sun is always high in the sky and it never rains. And a gryphon! They're one of the twelve Sacred Beasts who can speak like humans. They come into stories in the Sacred Mysteries." Then she grinned. "My old nurse used to tell me stories about them too; they're supposed to love gold and hoard it. I always wanted to see one."

I stood up. "Perhaps you will. But now I'd better train as usual. There's a festival when the Dance will be given in a few days, isn't there? I have a feeling about that."

Ariadne pouted a little. "All right, come this evening as usual, we'll talk again. But do you know why I'm sure it wasn't just a dream we all had? Not the pebble you put so much stock in. You could have picked that up anywhere. It's you, Britomartis. Your hair is more golden and you even look taller."

I smiled and shook my head at her, but I did feel stronger and lighter than I had ever felt. That day at training I did my first head leap on Winey and did it perfectly. It was that kind of day.

That evening Ariadne and I talked of the Path. "It always starts with that smoky tunnel," she said. "People often report seeming to be lost in it, trying to go one way and finding themselves going another. That's supposed to be what happened to Asteriako." She shuddered. "I've never heard of anyone being guided by a light before, or seeing any of the magical beasts. Usually anyone who goes to the Bright Land is brought there by a god or goddess who has some task or message for him or her. Sometimes people have come back blind or blasted as if by one of Diwa's thunderbolts. They say only those descended from gods can walk there."

"Daedalus claims that the family of Erechthoneus is descended from Hephaestus," I pointed out. "Almost as far back as yours is from Posudi. So if a god in your ancestry is all it takes you'd be as safe as I was. But don't you dare walk the Path while that priestess has anything to do with the gate. She meant to lose me in the Path all right and she wasn't a bit pleased when I came back. Where would I have gone if I had turned left?'

Ariadne shook her head. "I don't know. When I walked the Path I was simply told to go in and wait for a sign. I saw a goddess holding a tree in her hand; here she is on my seal. There was no background, just a sort of golden glow. She said, 'Wear my image on your seal, Ariadne. Go no farther for now.' Then she vanished and I was back in the tunnel. I followed the Thread of Life back to the Gate and told the priestess—the old one—my vision."

"Go no farther *for now*," I said.

Ariadne looked at me wide.eyed. "I never thought of that before," she said. "But it does sound as if she meant that I would come back sometime and go farther."

I pondered. "Do you know what goddess it was?" I asked.

Ariadne shook her head. 'That's puzzling too. It should have been Ria, since I belong to her, but she didn't seem to fit my idea of Ria. And I've never heard of Ria carrying a tree as a symbol."

"Perhaps Leto," I suggested dubiously. "Didn't she hold onto a palm tree on Delos when she bore Apollo and Artemis?"

Ariadne shook her head. "It wasn't a palm tree."

I stood up and looked out over the valley. I had eaten my evening meal with her for once and we were on the terrace sitting late over our food and wine. "When you loaned me your Veil of Adis and I made the others believe I was a goddess so easily I wondered if all the stories about gods and goddesses had started like that. The Veil is mysterious of course, but not as hard to believe in as the stories they tell about the gods. But I saw the gryphon. And you saw the goddess. You have the Veil and I have the gryphon feather. The world is stranger than I thought. And I'm sure we'll see stranger things yet."

I spoke more truly than I guessed. The next morning the news was all over the palace. M'nos was on his way back to N'sos and with him, apparently high in favor, was Astariano, the son of M'nos's wife and a bull who may have been a god.

Chapter Eight: M'NOS

For those of us in the know the arrival of M'nos hung like a dark cloud over that day. Ariadne and I, of course, waited to see whether what we had done so far would be secure and what counterstroke M'nos would have. Alceme was already building her own circle of Kaphtui friends and had some idea of what his arrival might mean. And what Alceme and I knew, Glaukos and Menesthius could at least guess, so close had the four of us become. For the ground dancers it was just another day of drill but the Leapers were nervous and as sometimes happens this made our performance better. We had never worked so well or so smoothly together and this pleased me until I saw unfamiliar faces among the spectators. At least some of those would be members of M'nos's court who had come back with him and would report our progress. And the greater that progress the greater the chance of our being put in the places of the present Dancers. As novices I can say without boasting that we were very good indeed, but we were not ready for that.

I expected M'nos to let us stew for awhile and he did; It was not until the afternoon of the day after his return that I was summoned to his presence. He was not in the big room where public business was done and where the stone replica of a captain's chair was set, but in a smaller room near the royal family's quarters. But he was seated on one of the several wooden captain's chairs that were used around the palace. On land only M'nos himself could use such a chair and whenever he sat on one became the throne chamber of the palace. By sitting in his chair he declared his intention of giving judgment or transacting the business of the kingdom.

Kaphtui are not orientals and no great ceremony is used in the presence of M'nos, nor does he receive the salute that I had been given by N'suto in the harbor. That is saved for goddesses and priestesses. But his own troops and officials give him a similar salute: the fist is raised to the forehead, thumb in. It is the same salute sailors give their captain and I was used to seeing it on the ship and when I was ushered before the dark slender figure on the familiar high-backed captain's chair I gave it without thinking. But the act of doing so gave me an idea and when he looked at me without speaking I said "Kariase, the leader of the novices, at your command, King M'nos."

His eyes, I saw, were gray though his hair was almost as dark as Ariadne's. His skin was as deeply tanned as P'sero's and the pale eyes in the dark face were disconcerting. He made no sign but I knew he had understood every implication of my greeting from the Kaphtul form of my name to my identification of myself as the leader of the novices, and my offer of service. His reply, in Kaphtui, was gravely courteous. "You are the daughter of Lykos, son of Pandion, are you not, Lady?" I bowed my head in assent, and he spoke to his attendants without taking his eyes from my face. "A chair for the Athenian princess."

A low-backed chair from an adjoining room was brought in quickly and quietly and I sank into it with a murmured, "Thank you, my Lord." I wondered whether I was being flattered or mocked.

One thing was certain, nothing the man did was direct or simple. At first glance he could have been as young as his daughter, there was no gray in his hair. But though he was still lithe and slender there were deep wrinkles around his eyes and the lines from his nose to the corners of his mouth were deep. It was an intelligent face, even a wise one, and clearly the face of one accustomed to command and to assert his will. But there was something else about him, something that made me uneasy. There was about him a faintly withered quality as if he had been exposed to some force too strong even for his will and it had sapped and drained his humanity. Something about him reminded me just a little of the ring I had flung down in Daedalus's workshop and even of the priestess who had tried to lose me on the Path.

This impression was somehow confirmed when he said in a colorless voice, "Your father is a great craftsman, Lady. Some of his work is in the house I have just come from." The words were kind but they were spoken without warmth. And he had not said that he owned or admired the work he spoke of, only that it was in the house—Rhadamantes's house—he had come from. I nodded in response to his remark but did not speak. It was not for me to praise my father's work and certainly it was not for me to deprecate it.

He sat up slightly, like one who comes to business after social preliminaries which are gone through only as a matter of form. "How are the novices shaping. Lady?" he asked.

I answered without hesitation. "Well, my Lord. When the time comes they will be ready to catch their bull and take their place as Dancers." My pieces were on the board now, as the Kaphtui would say. By my words I was telling him that I expected the Athenians to be treated like the novices of any other year.

His next words seemed to accept this. "Are any of you ready to take part in the Dance of this year as novices?"

I replied, "None in my charge are ready yet." I would not lie but I would evade as long as I could.

His countermove was instant: "And yourself, Lady?"

I made my last evasion. "That is for my trainers to say."

He had me at bay now and he knew it. "They say you are ready." He went on gravely, reasonably. "As you know, Lady, my son met his death from a bull. I would no longer have the Lady Ariadne put herself at risk, despite her great skill. It is my will that she withdraw from the Dance and that you take her place for the remainder of the year. When you tell me your companions are ready I will replace the Lady Ph'dare and my two nephews who are Leapers with your Leapers." He knew, of course, every detail of the traditions of the Dance: to replace all the Leapers was unusual but not completely unprecedented. And the effect was to put four Athenians in the positions of greatest danger.

He had one last stroke. "In the Spring you will hunt your own bull and all will go on as it always has. The next group of Athenians will come as soon as the seas are safe for sailing in the Spring, and become the new novices." The effect of this would be that our Leapers would serve a year and a half instead of the usual year, and then be replaced by Athenians. Early training of novices has always started in midwinter and many of the festivals at which the Dance was performed were still ahead in late summer and autumn. The next group of Athenians was a problem for the future. First we must survive until winter. I bowed my head. "As you will, M'nos."

"So be it," he said and, clever as he was, he said it a little too loudly. I knew it was a signal.

From a doorway in my line of sight a young man stepped forth, a handsome, saturnine young fellow with a marked resemblance to M'nos. Standing in the doorway, he looked at me fixedly. I heard a suppressed gasp from one of the attendants in the room but all I saw was a young man, a bit too elaborately curled and bejeweled, standing staring at me from a doorway.

M'nos spoke in a voice devoid of all expression. "My son, Astariano. I think you have not met him yet, Lady."

I nodded courteously to Astariano. "He has a great resemblance to you, M'nos."

I was quite sincere. It was merely a remark made to say something, a conventional remark to a father about a son. But it shook M'nos's self-control and for a second I saw a glare of genuine hatred from his eyes. Then he was in control again.

"Astariano is the son of my wife; she was my sister. Since my own son is dead, I have taken Astariano in his place. His parentage is divine."

I looked at the young man and said, "The children of the gods are blessed." This time I was being deliberately provocative; the Kaphtui word for "blessed" that I used is only used in connection with Olympians, not in connection with Those Below.

Astariano's lips drew back in a snarl but M'nos's voice was colorless again as he said, "Thank you, Lady. My son and I have matters to discuss and you will excuse us."

I rose, bowed, and went toward the door I had come in. I did not salute again. That salute and the offer of service it implied, had been sincere, but I felt relieved of any allegiance by what had passed. Under all his polite words M'nos had been saying, "I am your enemy. I will destroy you if I can, and I can."

The next moment my own self-control was strained to the limit, for Ariadne was standing just outside the door wearing the Veil of Adis. I continued on out as if she were not there and then as I turned a bend in the corridor outside that concealed us from the throne room I felt the coldness behind me and found myself with Ariadne under the Veil; she had lifted it and cast it over me, too.

"Walk as close as you can," she whispered, "the Veil will cover two, but only just." We were fairly near her room. When we reached the anteroom Ariadne touched the shoulder of an older lady in waiting who

94

had a noble face worn by sorrow. The woman got up and took a folded cloth into Ariadne's room, then went out again with a different piece of cloth. We slipped into the room behind her and waited until she closed the door behind her.

"M'riata knows about the Veil," said Armadne. "If ever you cannot find me, go to her. She can be trusted." She had pulled the Veil off of us and was folding it away. I wondered if the Veil itself was visible to Ariadne and if not how she found it when she needed it. She turned to me. "What did you see when Astariano came in?"

I shrugged. "A rather insolent young man. Older than I thought."

Ariadne shook her head. "He's a year and a half younger than I am. About your age. He's always looked older than his age. He was never a real child, even as a baby. But I didn't see his face." She shuddered. "His body was all right but his head seemed to be the head of a bull."

I stared at her. "The head seemed a little smoky and unsubstantial," she said. "Maybe that was the veil or maybe your true sight is rubbing off on me. It always looked solid when we were children."

I burst out, "He's produced this—illusion—before?" I asked.

She nodded. "Only once or twice, when he was really angry and wanted to frighten someone into fits. He tried it on Andaroko and me once, but Andaroko just knocked him down. He was never afraid of anything." She went on after a pause. "They say the gods can really change their bodies into the form of beasts, not just in illusion. But I always thought that head was an illusion and your true sight proves it."

She began to laugh, slightly hysterically. "My father nearly went mad when you said Astariano looked like him. He thought you were seeing the bull's head, of course, and just had magnificent self-control. He'll admire you for that even though he'll hate you for defeating him. It would never occur to him that you meant it quite literally. Astariano does look like father. But what you said about the gods' children was deliberate, wasn't it?"

I smiled grimly. "Yes, by that time I knew they were trying some kind of trick and was ready to give as good as I got. I'm sorry your father hates me, Ariadne."

She sat on the bed and stared ahead of her. "He hates me too," she said in a small voice. "Because I wouldn't marry Andaroko. He wanted to see his son on the throne. You heard what he said about putting Astariako in the place of Andaroko. If he even suggests my marrying Astariano It will be open war between us. But I think he knows that. Ph'dare might do it. I suppose I'll have to watch my food for poison." She looked at me with tears in her eyes. "I loved my father when I was small, even took his side against my mother. But she was never well after giving birth to Astariano, and when she died he turned to the Powers Below. He got great power—that's how he made Aegeus give in. But you see what its done to him."

I nodded. "There's a kind of—darkness—about him."

She stood up and ran her fingers through her hair. "Let's get back to the practice field. I need air and exercise, and you need all the practice you can get. He told you, didn't he, that you have to take my place?"

I nodded. "Yes, and the other Leapers too, as soon as they're ready."

She touched my arm. "Don't worry about them for a while. He'll let us give them time to train, if only because all of his hatred of the Athenians is focused on you now. He doesn't believe you're ready and with anyone else he'd be right. But you were always good, and since you walked the Path you've been even better. I'm not really worried about your first Dance though you mustn't be overconfident. What worries me is what he'll do when he finds out how good you are."

I went to the door with her. "We'll worry about that when it happens. Won't anyone wonder about me coming out of a door I didn't go in?" She shook her head. "M'riata sent all of the other ladies on errands while I was gone. They'll assume we came in while they were gone. I wouldn't have used the Veil but you might have been followed and I needed to talk to you right away." We went out onto the practice field then and forgot our worries in drill; the sincerity of M'nos's concern for his daughter's safety was sufficiently shown by the fact that he had not forbidden her to practice.

The atmosphere of the palace began to change; some Kaphtui who had been friendly suddenly seemed distant or hostile. But everyone concerned with the Dance became friendlier toward the Athenians. By using the Dance to attack us M'nos attacked the Dance, and those who served the Dance drew a protective cloak around us. But even among the servants of the Dance someone must have served M'nos first and the Dance second, for on the morning of my first Dance I found the stone seal I had gotten from Daedalus missing when I awoke. A stranger could not have cut it from its thong without awakening me, it must have been one of the maid servants who saw to the needs of the girl novices and cleaned our room. They were always in and out of our rooms; privacy, as I said, was hard to get in the House.

I sped to Daedalus's workshop and told him what had happened. He gave me a saturnine look. "And someone from M'nos came last night for all my seal stones. M'nos wants to examine them. So it's lucky, isn't it, that I worked all night to finish this?" He held out my pebble, carved with the great crowned gryphon biting the snake, their bodies twisted so that the design filled the space of the pebble's face with lovely curves. "Your piece of rock kept dulling my best tools," be said severely.

"Thank you, Uncle," I said, for once giving him a hug and a kiss on the cheek.

As I ran out of the room he called after me, "Take care this afternoon."

Ariadne ate her food with the novices at noon and we talked quietly through siesta. Then she went to put on her robes and I went down to the practice field wearing a new kilt and belt, presents from Ariadne, with my new seal on a short cord around my neck, nestling in the hollow of my throat. Wearing it gave me the same light happy feeling I had had the day after walking the Path. The Dancers were lined up ready for the procession and the bull was already out, stamping and twitching, and pulling against the ropes around his horns, which were covered with flowers so that from a distance it looked as if he was held only by garlands of flowers.

Ph'dare stepped forward. "I claim my sister's place," she said defiantly but uncertainly.

It would have served her right to let her take it but I had the others to think of. "The power is the right," I said. "Quiet the bull."

She bit her lip and stepped back, knowing better than to try. I walked over and put my hand on Winey's shoulder; he snorted, ducked his head and nuzzled me, then stood quiet. I could feel power streaming into my chest and down my arm from the seal, and Winey seemed like an extension of my own body.

"Drop the ropes," I told the attendants. They looked astonished but obeyed. I took a real garland of flowers from an attendant and wound it around the great horns, keeping one loop in my hand. Even without the direct contact I could feel the ripple of Winey's muscles as he shifted his stance. I nodded to the Dancers and they fell into two lines. We started for the South Gate.

The entrance to the Great Court at N'sos is the hardest of any of the palaces: you actually take the bull down the long corridor which I had run along the night that I walked the Path. There is an awkward turn at the beginning and another just before you come into the court itself.

Right inside the entrance a man was standing. Astariano. Winey and I looked at him with complete indifference. I don't know if he tried any of his tricks; linked to me as he was, Winey would see what I saw.

"Only Dancers here,". I said with calm authority. "Move away." He fell back, looking astonished and gaped after us as the procession went into the corridor. We could hear the chanting from the court; the preliminary ceremonies. Then as the voices fell, we stepped out onto the Great Court of the House of N'sos.

Chapter Nine: THE GOD

The court was completely transformed; empty of everyone except M'nos and Ariadne on their thrones at the far end. But every door and window was packed with people; behind barriers at ground level and hanging over balconies and out of windows at the upper levels. These were nobles and officials; the servants were on the roofs, pushing and jostling for a good view so that it was a miracle that no one fell. The court was covered ankledeep with shredded bark from trees; there were special rooms to hold this bark, which was reused, and to keep it from getting damp. The dark bark gave the court a somber appearance; empty of people it looked somehow smaller, not larger.

We paced slowly down the court to the chanting of priestesses and the sound of flutes. About halfway down I saw a stirring in the bark: M'nos's last stroke. I stopped Winey with my mind; he wouldn't even have felt a tug on the garland. I leaned over and picked up the snakes; two large house snakes from some shrine. Snakes are simple creatures, a slight flow from my seal put both to sleep and I put one around my neck and held the other, in my hand.

We continued our slow pacing to a buzz from the crowd. Only the closest spectators. could see that the things I had picked up were snakes but everyone had seen me pause. I went up to the thrones, closer than the ceremony called for, but I intended to give the snakes to Ariadne. She took them as if this were an everyday part of the ceremony; of course, as a priestess of Ria she was used to holding snakes at various ceremonies. As they left my hands they woke up; she used her own powers to make them coil around her arms and go to sleep again. There was a gasp from the nearer spectators when they realized the snakes were alive.

I looked calmly into M'nos's pale eyes, gave the salute the ceremony called for and turned Winey. The flutes signaled the beginning of the Dance proper. Kom'ku, the Leaper who was Ariadne's partner, stepped to the other side of Winey while the others danced their way into two long lines. Kom'ku and I led the bull down the Dance while the ground dancers and the other Leapers wove in and out in an intricate pattern which gave way before us as we walked the bull back down the court and closed in behind us. When we reached the south end of the court, we turned the bull again.

The handlers were waiting at the entrance to the court; normally they would have stepped out and taken the ropes. But I shook my head slightly and they fell back. I gave a pull to the garland and it fell apart. There was another gasp and buzz as the nearer spectators passed on to the ones farther away that the bull had been held only by a garland. Winey stood free, quivering now with excitement but completely under my control as I turned my back on him and danced back through the pattern with Kom'ku. That was the hardest part of the whole afternoon. The steps were not second nature then and I had to keep hold of Winey's mind.

When we reached the end of the court near the thrones, though not nearly so close to them this time, Kom'ku fell to the side and I stood alone in the middle of the court and called Winey to me. The first run was supposed to be very much the same sequence Ariadne had showed me in my first sight of the Dance; a vault, two single side handstands and the swing on the horns by two girls, followed by my head leap. The vaults and stands went as usual, but when it came time for the swing on the horns Ph'dare, who was one of the two who did this leap, did not move. Her partner checked; of course a swing on one horn would be madness.

This swing on the horns was intended to bring the head down and slow the bull. Without it the head leap would be harder, though not impossible, since I could dip Winey's head and slow him by using my power. I dipped his head but did not slow him much; I was sure I could handle the extra speed. As I ran toward the lowered horns time seemed to slow to a crawl; I seemed to have infinite time to get my grip just right. It was hard to tell in the lift what was my spring and what was Winey's toss. I landed solidly on his back and did a handspring off a standard jump except for the speed.

The hardest part of the head leap when you are tauromath is that it is done near the end of the bull's run and you must immediately think of turning him. But the fact that you are mind-linked to the bull means that he is conscious of you as you are of him, and as soon as you go over his back he begins to slow and get ready to turn. By running to the side to be ready for your side leap you pull his attention over to that side; he turns in that direction and begins his runback. It is then you must push him away with your mind so he runs straight down the court instead of diagonally toward you.

As I was accomplishing this I felt a flutter around the edges of my mind; someone was trying to take control of the bull from me. They hadn't a chance, of course. Ariadne might have done it if she had tried, after all, she had caught and trained Winey. But no other tauromath could have broken the link I had established with him. It was unusual even for one tauromath to be able to control another's bull well; the close link between Ariadne and me had helped me establish rapport with Winey.

Kom'ku and I did our side leaps, with that little check at the top of the handspring that makes it spectacular; two hurtling bodies frozen for an instant at the top of their swing over the bull's back. The next leaps in the Dance as it had been practiced were similar side leaps by two girls, Ph'dare and her partner. But this time Ph'dare had to leap alone; her partner did not move. I suppose it was her way of protesting Ph'dare's refusal to do the hornswing earlier. It was a lovely leap but Ph'dare and I both knew it would be her last. I could never trust her on the court with me again.

Toward the end of the court the strong man of the team did his handspring on the court, touched the bull's back with his feet and rolled in the air, landing on his feet again. He was a little thrown off by all that had happened and really needed the steadying hands of his partner for once; usually if you land well the hand touch is a formality. According to the Dance as rehearsed, Winey would go on out the corridor to be caught by the handlers. But I turned him again and ran lightly down the length of the court before he gathered speed. The others, not knowing what I was up to, stood still at the sides. I felt a little tug at my mind as I passed Ph'dare, but it was feebler than the previous attempt to break my link with Winey. Not, I thought, the same mind.

As I met Winey two-thirds down the length of the court, I went into a hand leap I had practiced in secret. As Winey's toss sent me over his horns, I twisted and landed on his back, facing his head. And as he thundered down the court I stayed on his back, every muscle straining for balance. Ariadne knew what I was doing; It was a story of hers about legendary feats of Leapers in the past that had given me the idea. But M'nos must have thought I had gone mad and would run the bull into the thrones. His self-control was total; he never moved a muscle.

As we neared the thrones there was a new problem as I brought Winey to a stop; I did not want him to skid stiff-legged, which would have looked undignified, but I did not want him to slow tamely to a trot either. In addition,I had to keep my balance as his pace changed. Gratefully I felt Ariadne's mind take hold with mine to help me slow Winey. He recognized her, of course, and would have swerved to avoid her even if he had been out of control. Just having her there would have helped to slow and stop him. I had counted on that.

As we reached a point directly in front of the thrones, Winey finally stopped. I did a slow controlled handspring over his horns and stood before M'nos, the bull's breath hot on my back, my head thrown back and my hands raised palm upward in the attitude of one who prays to the Olympian gods.

As I brought my eyes down my heart seemed to stop. Standing in front of a small shrine on the north wall of the court was a man's figure, taller by half a head than anyone I had ever seen. His long hair and beard were an intense blue-black and his face and body were deeply bronzed. There was a lazy smile on his lips. His eyes were green and his face was as wild, untamable and alien to humanity as the great sea itself. He was totally naked; very definitely male but somehow sexless. He gave a little nod when he saw that I saw him, then stamped his foot on the ground.

The hill underneath the House gave a little shudder and the whole House shook slightly, as if it shrugged and settled back. There was dead silence as M'nos rose to his feet, jerkily like a puppet. I wondered if the bearded giant held him as I held Winey.

"The god is pleased," said M'nos in a loud expressionless voice like that of a herald, then almost collapsed back into his chair.

The green-eyed giant lifted a hand in farewell and suddenly was no longer there. A few golden specks danced in the air for a moment, then vanished.

The crowd, which had been utterly silent from the time I leapt onto Winey burst into excited cheers. I felt

Kom'ku's arms around my waist and I was lifted to Winey's shoulders. Taking one of Winey's horns, Kom'ku turned him and led him down the court, with the Dancers weaving their pattern before and behind us again and the flutes pealing. Someone in the crowd called, "Atane!" and it became a rhythmic chant as we went down the court. "A-ta-ne! A-ta-ne!" We reached the corridor and went in. I slipped from Winey's back and let the handlers take him. Ph'dare went away, but the other Dancers were crowded around me, hugging me and congratulating me.

Some hours later I came out of a daze to realize that I was in the midst of a riotous party in the Dancer's quarters. There was a cup of wine in my hand and I think I had eaten something, but I had no real memory of anything since I had left the Court. Even later when I was more used to working the bull I found that this blackout sometimes occurred after the strain of controlling a bull. What had woken me out of my daze was T'ne, standing before me with snapping eyes, her hand on the arm of Ph'dare's partner. "She told me that it wasn't planned. You didn't tell them not to do the hornswing. Ph'dare refused. I thought you were showing off and I was furious with you, but now I know it was Ph'dare."

I shook my head, hugged Ph'dare's partner to show her I knew it was not her fault and sent her away. I turned to T'ne. "Don't worry about Ph'dare; she has punished herself. She will never Dance again. If you want to help me, spend all the time you can on Alceme: I'll need at least her for the next Dance."

T'ne nodded calculatingly. "She will be good with a little more drill. She loves admiration; now that she's seen how the crowd reacts she'll never rest till she can do a head leap too."

I grinned. T'ne knew Alceme very well. I gave T'ne a one-armed hug with the hand which didn't have the wine cup and looked around the room for Ariadne. She was sitting on a bench at the end of the room talking quietly to P'sero and I went toward them.

P'sero rose, gave me a bear hug and rumpled my hair. "You sail that bull like I sail my ship," he said, then nodded to Ariadne and went off.

Ariadne took my hands and we looked into each other's eyes for a moment, needing no words. We sat down and people left us to ourselves.

"You should be in bed," she said with mock severity. "Until you woke up just now I thought that Winey had given you his mind in exchange for yours." Only she and T'ne, of the people there, knew the aftereffects of controlling a bull, of course. Then she said wonderingly, "My father declared that the god was pleased!"

"He had no choice," I replied, "the god was pleased." She looked at me wide-eyed as I described the figure I had seen, then became excited. "But that means our troubles are at an end. He must know the god made him speak. He won't dare harm you now!" I hoped so, and I tried to look happy for her sake, but I had a sinking feeling that M'nos would not be so easily defeated.

The next day my fears seemed groundless. M'nos and Astarino had gone back to the summer palace, and those who had been hostile to us were suddenly friendly. A happy time followed, occupied with the technical problems of working Alceme, Glaukos and Menesthius into Ariadne's Dancers in place of Ph'dare and her two cousins. One of them was the strong man, and no one else could do that leap, so we had to rechoreograph the Dance. But we still had four of Ariadne's Leapers, and we could bring along my Leapers gradually.

Ph'dare had gone with her father and there seemed not a hostile face in the House. But we soon left N'sos, for the Dance goes on circuit in the autumn; it is danced at the Harvest Festival in each of the major palaces, ending with the Great Fall Festival at N'sos, which is the latest.

Ariadne went on tour with us and occupied the Queen's Chair at each Dance, next to the tributary kings who were M'nos's governors for each area. When we were at Ph'stos I wondered if M'nos would come down from T'suto, the House of the Three Kings; but he did not. The court and the Dance were always the same, excpt for minor local variations. M'lia has a stone altar in an awkward place in the court, for instance, and the pavement of the court at Ph'stos was in need of repair that year. But once the bark was on the court and the thrones set up, any court could have been the Great Court at N'sos.

We traveled slowly and in state. Winey walked and had to be rested before the Dance. At each palace we were feasted before and after the Dance; Ariadne as the Holy One of Ria and I as Mistress of the Dance were the guests of honor. At great feasts men and women eat together, and afterward do other things together, but as the Dancers must be virgins that was not our concern.

I tried no more bull riding and saw no more gods. I saved my ideas for new leaps for next year, when we would have only four Leapers and would have to do something good to make up for the smaller group. So it was largely the same Dance that Ariadne had choreographed for the Dancers of her year that we did, modified only to take account of the strengths and weakness of the new Athenian Leapers. Alceme did not put herself forward; she knew that she could not compete yet with the more experienced girls. Glaukos practiced the Roll Under, for he was too stockily built to fly over the bull, but with steady practice Menesthius was becoming a good all-around Leaper. Some of the other Athenian boys could have been trained but the other girls were hopeless and the team had to be balanced, like everything else in Kaphtu, by sexes.

Despite her still modest accomplishments as a Leaper, Alceme was getting her share of popularity. Partly this was due to her golden hair, even rarer in Kaphtu than on the mainland. Partly it was due to her figure; most girl Leapers are beanpoles like T'ne or at any rate boyish in figure. I was still fairly flat, and Ariadne's breasts though well-shaped were small. But bare breasts are commonplace in Kaphtu. It was our legs the male spectators looked at; for no woman but a Dancer bares her legs above the knee in Kaphtu, and our kilts left our legs exposed up to the hip bone.

Not that any man would have dared to lay a finger on a Dancer. I think this was a disappointment to

Alceme who was a lusty girl and in later life an enthusiastic mother. But she could always wait for her satisfactions, and had her eye out for a good marriage. Alceme really had less respect for men than I did, but she would rarely meet them head-on, as she had Euphoros that day: she preferred to rule them by traditional feminine means—guile and fascination.

Ariadne would now tolerate Alceme and even began to like her, Glaukos and Menesthius she treated like her own male Leapers, that is, like brothers. We formed a tight-knit little group of six, for the strong man Riatano son of Rhadamantes traveled with us and oversaw our arrangements; it had been his job when Ariadne had been Mistress of the Dance, and no one else had the experience to take his place.

So we were happy, pleased with ourselves and much too overconfident when we returned to N'sos for the break before the Great Harvest Festival.

Chapter Ten: THE TABLET

We were all constantly being laden with gifts. Any of us could have set up as a traveling jewelry trader on the jewels we were given, and we got gifts of food, clothing and any luxury you could name. But one morning after our return to N'sos a palace servant brought me something unusual: a small tablet of baked clay with twisting lines on its surface. Ariadne was busy with administrative duties that fell on her shoulders while her father was away, and I danced off to my next best source of information, Daedalus. As I entered his workroom after a perfunctory knock he looked up from some intricate piece of work. "And where are the other two Graces?" he inquired. It was his idea of humor to refer to Ariadne, Alceme and myself as the Three Graces. Ariadne with her dark vividness and Alceme with her blond loveliness fitted the name, but I felt that I, with my brown hair and my "big chin" lowered the standard.

"Ariadne's sitting in judgment," I replied, "and Alceme is talking to a friend of P'sero's about investing some of her jewels in an Egyptian trading venture."

Daedalus sighed. 'That girl has an eye to the main chance," he said. "She'll marry me if I don't watch out, and I like being a widower. It's a quiet life."

I cocked a skeptical eyebrow at him. "You could do worse," I said. "But she's looking for a younger man. She'd wear you out, Uncle." I put the tablet on his bench. "What is this?' I asked.

He puzzled over it, then pulled from his shelves a scrap of parchment with some lines on it, and consulted it. "It seems you own a flock of sheep, niece," he said. "Someone has given you the title to a wool flock. These scratches on parchment or clay are a way of keeping records. They do it in Egypt too." He pointed to a scribble. "See that's a sheep's head, and this is a number. The two bars mean male sheep; that's a flock of males kept for their wool; they can be grazed higher and rougher than a flock with ewes and lambs."

"What good is a flock of sheep to me?" I asked. "And where would I keep it?"

He shook his head disgustedly. "Don't be a fool, niece. The flock is up with the rest of them, in the charge of the king's shepherds. You get the wool after the shepherds are taken care of and new male yearlings gotten as replacements for old sheep that die. A flock is wealth that keeps coming in, not like jewelry. You can trade the wool for anything you like. You never see it; everything is done by marks in the king's accounts."

"Could I have a bathtub made?" I asked, "long enough to stretch my legs in?" He nodded, amused, and I had another idea. "Could I go see my sheep?'

He scratched his head. "I don't see why you'd want to, but no doubt it can be arranged. Talk to one of the king's stewards."

I trotted off and, being full of energy and with nothing to use it on, I soon had arrangements in train. A bathtub would be formed and fired by the potters, painted with dolphins and fired again; it should be ready in a handful of days. I had discovered the present location of my flock, borrowed a donkey and got directions, and was on the road by afternoon.

All this was possible because of the long gap between the last festival outside N'sos and the Great Harvest Festival at N'sos. The bull is being rested from the travels and given light exercise, and the Dancers too get a break if they keep in training. The gap is so long not because the harvest is so late at N'sos but because it is a Gathering In festival; it is held when all the wine and oil and grain are safe in M'nos's storerooms and written down in his accounts.

The autumn weather was still warm and it was good to be through with the stickiness at Kaphtu's humid summer. I rode out on my donkey full of excitement, after flinging excited explanations at Ariadne and the others; none of us thought of any danger. The person of a Dancer is sacred and I wore my kilt under a traveling cloak; even without it I was fairly well-known by face and figure to many Kaphtui. The soldiers at guard-points on the roads waved me past with a grin and even when I left the stone roads for the hill tracks I could usually see a guard-post on a distant hill.

I found the flock that evening with little trouble and as the light faded looked them over with the aid of an old shepherd who was childishly pleased that one of the great ones from N'sos should come and look at his charges. As we sat by his fire that evening eating a roasted lamb procured from nearby shepherds of a mixed flock he spoke in short, simple phrases of the beauty and hardships of wintering a flock in the hills. There were so many flocks that there was no question of taking them all to lowland pasture, even when snow came; they were kept as high as was safe and fed on whatever could be found for them. The wool flocks composed of mature males pastured hardest and highest.

Suddenly a dark figure loomed near the fire and the shepherd came back smiling and carrying a jug. "My friends down in the valley have sent up some good wine in your honor," he said. It was thick, sweet-smelling stuff but I choked it down to please him. He was so transparently honest I had no doubts of the wine, nor did I think to ask who these mysterious friends were who had palace wine up here in the hills. But the next morning I awoke with a thick head, and flock, shepherd and shepherd's hut were all gone, along with my donkey. I was lying near the mouth of a shallow cave in a little clearing cut in head-high thorny bushes, completely alone. All around me the thorn bushes were unbroken and impenetrable.

Whoever had moved me had lain me on several clean sheepskins, which was their first mistake. Aside from that there were bread and olives in jars and a big jar of water, a few cracked plates and cups and a large smelly jar for slops. There had once been a path cut through the thorn bushes but it had been filled in with cut bushes and new thorns had wound among them, welding them into an immovable mass. The cliff above the cave was sheer but not high; I wondered if I had been lowered from it to the clearing. It looked hopeless at first; the thorn bushes would tear your flesh if you tried to push them aside, and I had no tools to cut them. Even my little belt-knife had been taken.

I could use the gryphon feather, of course; it was still nestled in my hair as it had been ever since that day. But I had only three uses of that and this seemed too tame a trap to make use of it. Tame, but deadly; without hurting me at all they could destroy my Dancers by simply keeping me here till after the festival. I wondered who was responsible: M'nos, Astariano or could it even be Ph'dare? I put my mind to work on the problem of getting out; who had trapped me was of no present importance.

In the end, I found a solution I was quite pleased with. I laid a sheepskin on top of the bushes at their lowest point and jumped up onto it, carrying the other skins; no feat for a Dancer. The bushes were so tough they bore my weight easily. Then I simply laid a sheepskin ahead of me, crawled onto it and moved the first sheepskin ahead of me again. A smaller skin I wrapped around my hand to beat aside the occasional taller branch in my way. By the time I reached the spur of rock which formed the cliff with the cave I was glad I had paused for bread, water and olives before starting. I had to parallel the ridge for awhile before it fell away to a height I could scramble up. There was a path on it which I followed to the top of the cliff, where I flung the sheepsklns down to puzzle my former captors. Then I retraced the path to where it joined a hill path. I was guided by a barking dog to a familiar hut, not really all that far away.

The shepherd had left his dog in charge of my donkey. Whoever had moved me had not dared to touch my seal-stone: with its aid I quieted the dog and caught the donkey. The shepherd was no doubt reporting the disappearance of his visitor to the nearest guard-post. If M'nos was behind this the soldiers might know about it already because they might have been my captors. I wished I could calm the shepherd's fears. I had liked the old man. But I had no idea in which direction he had gone and thought it wisest to head straight back to N'sos.

However, my enemies were still a step ahead of me. As I rode the donkey over a trail carved out of a hillside high in the hills I heard the slipping of rock and gravel. This piece of trail, as I had seen from below, was bolstered up by great timbers and braces; someone had pulled or knocked out one of the braces ahead of us and the trail was sliding away; avalanching down into the valley below. Just then I heard the same sound behind and the ground shifted under my feet. I slid off the donkey and with a sudden panic-stricken leap he bounded ahead and, miraculously scrambling over the edge left of the trail ahead, he vanished around the bend.

I wondered if he could have done it with my weight on him and if I could get out the same way, but already the thin edge of trail he had used was sliding away. The ledge I was on felt none too stable and the cliff to the side of me was sheer. The drop below was too great even for someone used to leaping and tumbling; there was no stable ground to land on. I shrugged and pulled the gryphon feather from my hair, throwing it out into the air. Almost as soon as it left my fingers there was a golden flash and hovering in the air before me was the great gryphon himself. The feather was back in my hand and I thrust it in my hair again.

"Can you take me through to the Bright Land?" I called. This had been in my mind before; to make a call on the gryphon the occasion of another visit to that mysterious country.

He nodded and seized me gently with his great claws. One, two, three beats of his wings and there was another golden flash. The same hills were below us, it seemed, but with no trace of roads. The sun, which had been low in the sky and partly obscured with autumn haze, was directly overhead, a blazing summer sun. The mighty wings bent to gain height and then we glided toward the green hill which stood where the House rose in our world. We landed gently in the same hollow where we had first met.

I looked into those golden eyes and decided to risk a question. "If I walk from here to the cave I returned through before, will I get back to my own world by tomorrow morning?" That was an awkward way of putting it, but even aside from what Ariadne had told me I had the feeling that it was always noonday here and that "morning" would have meaning only in relation to my own world.

The gryphon's high remote voice replied, "Yes, if you do not tarry on the way."

I waited because I was sure that he would ask me a question in return, and I was right. But the question itself surprised me.

"Is Ariadne's hair the same color as Posudi's?"

I stared at him. "Y-yes," I stammered. How did he know that I had seen Posudi in the Great Court? Somehow I had never doubted it was Posudi, but hearing him say it shook me.

"I thought so," said the emotionless voice. He gave a spring into the air, there was a beating of wings and he dwindled into the sky.

I turned and started walking to the hills, my mind in a turmoil. The gryphon knew somehow that Posudi had appeared to me. But he didn't know the color of Ariadne's hair. That made sense in a way. Posudi was an inhabitant, presumably, of this world, and transactions between this world and mine could be of interest to other inhabitants of the Bright Land. But the inhabitants of this world might very well have limited knowledge of our world.

The question itself was a curious one. What concern was Ariadne's hair to the gryphon? What did the question mean? I suddenly stopped, struck by a possible explanation. What if Ariadne was not the daughter of M'nos at all? Her mother had cuckolded M'nos once, why not twice, or even three times? I wondered who Andaroko had resembled. I shook my head. There was no use speculating about these things now, and I was wasting precious time. I had wanted to walk from the hill where N'sos stood in our world to the cave for several reasons. First I wanted to try the effects of a longer exposure to the blazing sun of this land; I was beginning to have an idea about that. Second, I wanted to see all I could of this land, test it in every way I could.

In my own world I trusted my eyes implicitly, and with the Veil of Adis and with Astarianos attempts to frighten me I had received new confirmation that my eyes showed me what was truly there. But this place puzzled me and so did its inhabitants. No four-legged creatures in our lands flew or had both feathers and fur. Yet the shape of this land and, so far as I could see, its plants and trees, were just like those of our land. I was crossing the valley now which was cultivated land in the valley where N'sos stood, and I kept my eyes out for signs of cultivation. There were none. This might be a place where human beings had never lived. Yet the trees were much the same. I had passed olive trees and now I came near a small fig tree.

I looked at it, considering. The fruit was ripe, but none seemed overripe. There were no flies around the fruit and no wasps. Indeed, it struck me that I had seen no insects here and no birds unless the flying creature I had seen on my first entry to this world was a bird. Every sense told me this land was as real and solid as ours, and yet... But I had not tried every sense yet. With sudden determination I plucked a ripe fig and sunk my teeth in it. I am not extremely fond of figs, but this one was delicious. I ate every scrap of it and licked my fingers.

I tried to assess my reactions. Did I feel less hungry? Impossible to say. I couldn't imagine feeling hunger pangs here, or fatigue, or sorrow. Yet I didn't feel overfull either, as you do sometimes when you eat for taste without being hungry.

I walked on into the silent hills that lay between me and the sea. Nothing seemed to happen in this land: it lay passive under that blazing sun. It would have surprised me now to see a rabbit or a bird; rabbits and birds would mean birth and death and this land seemed alien to either. I wondered if I went back to the fig tree whether there would be a new ripe fig where I had plucked that one. What would happen if I ate every fig on the tree? I had set out to find some of the secrets of this land, but the face it showed me, though apparently open and candid, was completely inscrutable.

In what seemed a short time I was walking along the edge of the bay, on my way to the cave. It was frustrating to learn nothing more of this land, but I had to be back for the next Dance, and I didn't dare to linger. Then, when I had almost reached the cave, I saw another human figure on the beach. A young man in an ordinary Danaan tunic was walking toward me on the hard sand near the waves.

As he came closer I could see that his hair was dressed in Danaan style, and his face looked Danaan too, though not Attic. Something about him reminded me of Thebans I had seen in Athens. He greeted me with a broad grin. "A Cretan bull-girl! How did you get here, darling? Did you wander into the cave? You're surely too young to be asking Eluethia's help!"

As he spoke, something came stealing over me, a lightheadedness, a sweet languorousness. It was like being drunk and in the throes of infatuation at the same time. But I knew a little myself about mind influencing mind, and I summoned anger to my aid. Concentrating all my will and channeling it through my seal stone I pushed that influence away, and struck at him with my anger. It was no doubt a feeble slap to him, but he was not to know it was my best effort.

He took a step backwards, a hand raised as if to ward me off. "Your pardon, Lady. I didn't recognize..." He frowned. "I still don't. Who in the Halls of Hades are you?"

I smiled, quite composed now that he had stopped that insinuating attempt to influence me. "No one in the Halls of Hades, but here and in my own world I am Britomartis, called Chryseis."

He looked hard at me. "But you're too young. And she's..."

My heart leaped. He could only be speaking of my mother. But instinct told me I would get further by pretending to know more than I did.

"You must be thinking of my mother," I said, trying to appear casual. "You see my hair is darker, and as you say, I'm younger."

He was puzzled and a little suspicious. "But who is your father, then?"

I replied, as if it were something he should have known, "Lykos, son of Pandion, prince of Athens."

He snapped his fingers. "Of course! I've heard that story. We're much in the same boat then. My mother was Semele, Princess of Thebes." I longed to ask who his father was, but didn't dare reveal my ignorance. He smiled, a friendly grin now and not his seducer's smirk. "You may call me Dion. We have much in common. Can you talk awhile?"

I longed to, but knew any more of this riddling talk would soon reveal my ignorance. "I have an appointment with a bull. We'll meet again." I lifted my hand and walked into the cave, feeling his eyes on my back.

As I went around the pillar, always turning left, I wondered how essential this cave, or the ceremony that had first sent me here, was to passing between the two lands. Certainly Posudi had walked no Path to reach the Great Court or leave it. One moment he had been there and the next moment he had not been. When I had walked the Path I had seemed to see foggy walls. On my last trip through the cave it seemed to me that I had walked longer before the light changed and the shapes altered subtly. Was it possible to learn to go between the two lands without special aids? Did each time you went make it easier?

I walked toward the entrance to the cave, pale with the light of dawn, when I realized that I was not alone in the cave this time. A Kaphtui woman, heavily pregnant, was kneeling near the entrance. As she caught sight of me she cried, "Oh Bright Shining Lady! Oh Goddess! Help me!"

I stared at her, nonplussed, but as I looked down at her I saw that my hands and what I could see of the rest of my body did have a kind of glow or shine, visible even in the dawnlight coming through the cave mouth. It confirmed one of my suspicions about the power of the Bright Land and explained the woman's thinking I was a goddess, but how was I to answer her appeal?

In fact it was my suppliant who told me. "Bright Lady," she said, "the child in my womb has been growing feeble; it no longer moves as it did. If you would only lay your hands on me...

I could see how that might work. Heat can be transferred from one thing to another by contact; why not this power that seemed to pour into one from the sun of the Bright Land? I put my hands on her swollen stomach. Pregnant Kaphtui women wear a sort of loose gown, but she opened this as I bent toward her. Her flesh was warm but there was a subtle feeling of wrongness coming from somewhere inside. I concentrated on my hands, thinking of the power and the lightness and joy that I had felt on the day I returned for the first time from the Bright Land, trying to transmit that through my hands to the child in her womb.

I don't know how long I stood there with my hands on her. There seemed to be a sort of blankness in my mind as there had been after controlling the bull for the first time.

When I became aware of myself again the woman was repeating, "Oh thank you, my Lady, thank you. I can feel that it is well with the child again. I can feel it move." She had not looked at my face before: now she did, but her eyes were obscured by tears. I turned to go but felt I should say something. Curiosity took over.

"How did it happen?" I asked. "Have you been taking care of yourself?"

She nodded and gulped, "Yes, my Lady, everything the wise women said, I did. But one day I went to N'sos and the Lord Astariano brushed me aside when I was slow in getting out of his way. Ever since…"

I felt a spasm of pure rage. Astariano again. "Stay near home till the child is born," I told her. "It should be soon." Then I left the cave.

As I walked down the streets of Amnisos someone fell into step beside me: Dion. Had he followed me through the cave or could he move between the two lands without it? He spoke as if continuing a conversation. "I wouldn't have thought that you were the type to like to play goddess." When I looked at him without speaking, he went on with irritation in his voice. "How do you know what you've done by saving her brat? It may be born deformed or an idiot anyway. And you've used all the power you saved coming by way of the cave, have you thought of that?"

I stored this piece of knowledge in my mind. So one "saved power" by coming through the cave. As opposed to what, I wondered. Coming "directly" somehow? I shrugged. "She needed my help. I had it to give. It's what my mother would have done." That was true, and though I remembered it now for the first time in many years, pregnant women had often come to my mother, though she was not a midwife. As a child I had vaguely supposed she had given them advice or comfort; I wondered now if I had been unconsciously imitating something she might have done.

I thought it time to change the subject. "Since no one is staring at you, I presume you don't look like a

Theban to them. I don't see illusions so you'd better tell me what you look like to them."

He measured me with narrowed eyes. "Don't see illusions?" He picked up a nut from under a tree planted in a pot outside a house, and held it in his hand, concentrating, then opened his hand slowly.

I looked into his palm, astonished. "Why you made it sprout! The nut has opened and there's a tiny plant in it!"

He smiled a little sheepishly. "You were supposed to see a good-sized tree. You're right, you don't see illusions."

I looked into his face inquiringly. "But the sprout is there. That's real," I said.

He nodded. "Oh yes, you can make seeds grow until they use up their nourishment. And it's always better to have something real as the basis of an illusion."

He smiled at me. "I look like any other Cretan youth to them. Narrow waist, tight belt, hair in ringlets. What they expect to see, more or less." He looked around him. "I haven't been in a seaport for awhile. I think I'll have a look around. When is your bull dance?"

I raised an eyebrow. "This afternoon. Will you come?"

He grinned. "Oh, yes. I'll be there. Don't worry, I'll play no tricks. Posudi is jealous of that dance of yours." Then he wandered off down a side alley looking about him as if at an entertainment. A strange and irritating young man, with a wildness behind his eyes which was a little frightening.

Chapter Eleven: THE DEMON

I found when I reached the House that my friends
were anxious. Apparently the donkey I had borrowed
had come back to its pasture last night, with scrapes
and bruises on its body. Ariadne had sent messengers
looking for me on the road I had taken, and T'ne had
been preparing to take my place despite M'nos's
certain disapproval, and the break with the tradition of
the Dance. After thanking her warmly I drew her aside.
"T'ne, was there ever any gossip about the parentage
of Ariadne or her brother?" I asked.

She considered. "I've never been much interested
in gossip and of course I'm only a year or so older than
Ariadne. But I remember my mother saying that there
were no children for a long time after M'nos married
Ariadne's mother. The family is inbred, of course, with
all these brother-sister marriages and either of them
could have been sterile. Men always blame the woman,
of course, but if P'sephae thought it was M'nos, I can
imagine her taking lovers. But I don't think there was
ever any gossip about a particular man or men."

Sometimes T'ne's robust common sense was
cheering, other times it was a little off-putting. Most
Danaans would call childlessness in a brother-sister
marriage the wrath of the gods, but T'ne's father was

an official in charge of herds and flocks, and she saw very little mystery in breeding or birth. Still her explanation was likely enough. Some men, for whatever reason, could not seem to produce children with any woman. It was true enough that the woman was often blamed and that her recourse could be to prove her fertility by taking a lover. In Kaphtu, where women were free, that would not even be frowned on, but I could imagine M'nos being enraged if P'sephae was unwise enough to taunt him with what she had done. It would explain much about M'nos's relation to his wife and his daughter.

The immediate problem, however, was tonight's Dance. For the moment I simply told Ariadne that there had been attempts to delay me which had not succeeded, and I would tell her about it that evening. Then I called a hasty practice and spent some time with Winey. By the time we assembled for the procession we had slipped back into our familiar routine. I did not try to repeat my spectacular ride toward the thrones, but since this was the last Dance of the season, I ran Winey back and forth and back again, letting each Leaper do his or her best leaps; for Ariadne's remaining four this would be their last Dance. But as I turned Winey for the last time after my second leap I stayed in his path instead of going to the side and did a third head leap with the twist I had used before, riding down the court standing on Winey's back. I dropped off as we came to the corridor, and gave Winey's massive neck a hug as the handlers took him.

As with the Dancers who were the remnants of Ariadne's fourteen, this was Winey's last dance. The bull is not sacrificed after the Dance except at the funeral games of a king. Winey would go out to close pasture with his own harem of cows, protected from the younger bulls on the open range. The bull chosen for the Dance is supposed to be the best bull of his year, but while he is in the Dance, younger bulls take over in the range herds, and a bull broken to the Dance is no longer used to the competition with the other bulls. So to preserve his stock this arrangement is made; it probably owes something too to the fondness of Dancers for the bull they have trained and worked with.

M'nos had been in his throne for the dance; it was unthinkable for him not to be there for the Harvest Festival, but there was no repetition of any of the tricks that had been played at my first Dance. If Astariano was in N'sos there was no sign of him. Ariadne had ordered a special feast for the Dancers in one of the smaller banqueting halls of the house. It soon became a noisy party like the one after my first dance, though I was in better shape to observe it. I had not seen Dion during the Dance. You have no time to look for faces in the crowd if you are tauromath. But he was at the feast, making himself agreeable to everyone. Everyone assumed that he was the guest of someone else. If he had been challenged, I would have claimed him as my guest, but he was not. Once when I thought the gaiety was getting more hectic than could be explained by the amount that had been drunk I cast a suspicious giance in his direction. He met it blandly, but the party quieted.

So it was late and we were all tired when our little group of six were alone after the party. I told them briefly of the two attempts to delay me, describing my strategy with the sheepskins, but giving the impression that I had scrambled off the undermined road after the donkey. The consensus of our group was that Ph'dare was responsible; the traps were too clever for Astariano but not quite clever enough for M'nos. In this we may have underestimated Astariano or overestimated M'nos, but at any rate it was clear that whoever it was had not dared to harm me directly and had only hoped to delay me until it was too late to get to the Dance. Since the Dance was over for the year it seemed we could relax, but none of us were happy about the coming winter, with M'nos in residence at N'sos.

Riatano, the former "strong man" Leaper of Ariadne's Dancers, offered a solution. "Now that I am no longer in the Dance," he said, "M'nos will be obliged to redeem an old promise and give me the place of my father, Rhadamantes, as ruler of Ph'stos. As soon as I am confirmed in the position, I will invite Ariadne to visit me and propose to Chryseis as Mistress of the Dance that she bring her novices, now Dancers, to Ph'stos for winter training. Unless M'nos chooses to interfere with the training of the Dancers, which he has not done so far, Chryseis's consent is enough. We will all be together at Ph'stos for the winter out of the shadow of M'nos."

This sounded too good to be true, but in the event it worked out quite well. M'nos, I was sure, still wanted to destroy the Athenians, but his obsession was to destroy them by means of the Dance. So though he could have had us killed or harassed in a thousand different ways he was willing to wait for next year's Dances. At the same time he was no fonder of us than we were of him, and was just as glad to have us out of his sight. So no objection was made to the Dancers' move to Ph'stos.

Ariadne should really have been at N'sos for some of the winter ceremonies, but she too was able to come to Ph'stos without opposition from M'nos. She told me that he asked her bluntly if she was thinking of Riatano as a husband, but when she assured him she was not, he made no objection to the visit. I couldn't imagine her choosing Riatano as a husband and said so. She gave a little chortle of amusement. "Yes, poor Riatano, he's as strong as a bull, but his mind is like a bull's too." That wasn't really fair to Riatano who had always been competent and reliable in dealing with arrangements for the Dancers, and I told her so.

She nodded more soberly. "I didn't mean that he was stupid exactly, but he goes straight at things like a bull and he's easily enraged and as easily fooled or distracted. There'd be no surprises living with a man like that. I have a problem, Britomartis. I don't want to live with a man I can't respect or who doesn't respect me. But when I choose a husband I choose the next M'nos. He must be someone the nobles and the people will accept. For myself I might be content with Menesthius. He has a quick mind and he's gentle and considerate. But he'd never be accepted as M'nos. Riatano would probably be accepted, but I don't want him as a husband, and he's too simple to make a good ruler."

My own feelings about marriage were highly confused. My ideal of marriage, I suppose, was based on my own mother and father; they had been companions as well as lovers and had treated each other as equals. They had had occasional quarrels, but I couldn't imagine my father striking my mother or my mother tricking him into doing what she wanted by using tears or feminine wiles. But most Danaan husbands would think as little of beating a wife as of beating a slave, and most Danaan wives who were not totally submissive had very much the attitude Alceme had: a husband was someone to be managed and out-maneuvered for your own advantage.

I had seen less of Kaphtui husbands and wives. I was too young then to appreciate the depth of affection under the placid surface of P'sero's marriage; it seemed to me to be middle-aged and stodgy, with the excitement gone from it. The court ladies seemed to live a sort of communal life with husbands very much in the background. That seemed silly to me; why marry at all if you were going to see that little of your husband? Taking lovers was not frowned on in Kaphtu, but husbands seemed little but more official and permanent lovers.

I had no interest in lovers myself; I was slow to develop both physically and emotionally. But my encounter with Dion had made me aware of certain possibilities in myself that I had never realized; not in relation to Dion, whom I still distrusted, but in relation to someone, sometime. I had told Ariadne of what had really happened to me, of course, as soon as we could find time to be alone, and she was intrigued by Dion.

"If you say I talked to him at the feast, Britomartis, I must have," she told me. "I do vaguely remember a strange young man who seemed to know you and who was very easy to talk to. But I can't remember what he looked like. You've never seen him again?"

I had not. After the party Dion was simply gone, nor did I catch any glimpse of him in the days before our departure from N'sos. He had either gone back to the Bright Land or was keeping out of sight somewhere in Kaphtu. After we all moved to Ph'stos I didn't expect to see him and he soon went out of my thoughts, though I occasionally puzzled over him. But he had given me some ideas about the Bright Land and the gods which I argued with Ariadne and with Menesthius, who had been taken partly into our confidence about my experiences. When the three of us began our debates about the nature of gods, Glaukos, Alceme and Riatano were soon bored and wandered off, which made it easier for the three of us to speak freely.

My thinking on this matter had been started by my father, who was the only man or woman I had ever known who pondered such things rather than merely accepting them. I argued, as he had, that the Olympians were too human-like and limited to be responsible for all the things that happened in the world.

"I don't deny that Posudi can cause an earthquake. I have very good evidence for that," I said. "But if he is in the Great Court watching the Dance, how can he be ruling the sea too or causing an earthquake in Asia?

My father always argued that the gods must be akin to humans, since gods could have children with women and goddesses with men. "You know that even horses and donkeys only produce mules when they breed, as close as they are. And a dog and a donkey can't breed at all."

There was some ribald comment on this—our discussions were serious but not solemn—and I went on. "All right then, if they're akin to humans they have at least some human limitations. I don't see how they can be everywhere at once, or know everything. And certainly they're not always fair or just, to each other or to us, if the stories the poets tell are to be believed."

Menesthius intervened. He was always our defender of orthodoxy, though sometimes with very unorthodox arguments. "But what if the gods merely take the form of men to appear to us? And why trust the stories poets tell. What do they know of the gods' true nature?"

I shook my head, "But Menesthius, all we have are those stories. All the rituals, all the festivals are based on them. And I'm willing to grant that they're based on some reality. About their appearing to be men and women, I don't know. The only creature I've met that gave me the feeling that he might be only appearing to be what he seemed was my gryphon. If he had turned into a god in human form, or into something unimaginable I somehow wouldn't have been surprised. But I can't understand how a greater being could be content to take the form of a lesser one for any length of time. All these stories about Posudi running around as a horse or a bull—how would you like to be a bull for a year? And as for mating with a woman in bull form..." Here the discussion became rather earthy, since we had all observed the mating habits of bulls, and the discussion of the gods was dropped for then. But that discussion was to come back to us in a curious way.

We had all observed the mating of bulls because it was part of the winter training of a Dancer. Each group of Dancers must catch their own bull, and the bull was caught with a cow as decoy. While the bull was mating his feet were hobbled and ropes were thrown over him. Then the struggle to subdue him began. There had been few injuries in the Dance itself for many years, but many a Dancer was hurt in capturing the bull. This was largely due to the fact that with a new, wild, bull the tauromath could be of only very limited help. The link between bull and tauromath had to be built up over a long period and until it was established control of the bull was chancy and sometimes impossible. The cow was useful not only as a decoy but because after coupling the bull was in a less irritable state and easier to control.

There were certain traditional limitations on what means could be used to capture the bull, going back to the days when the Dance was a sort of test of strength and courage for the children of the reigning king, establishing their fitness to rule. Because the throne descended through the female line, the daughters of the king had to be part of the test, and thus the Ariadne was always a Dancer, though not always the Mistress of the Dance. That almost always went with being tauromath. T'ne had been Mistress of the Dance in her year.

In early times the Dance had been held only in special years, then every seven years, and now it was held yearly, for it had become a popular entertainment as well as an important religious ritual. With fourteen Dancers to be chosen every year there was no question, of course, of all of them being literally the king's children. But up to now all of them had had some relation, however remote, to the current M'nos; for example, T'ne's great-grandfather had been a brother of the M'nos of his time.

Most of the rules for catching the bull went back to quite remote times, but had been gradually modified. "Ropes and sticks" had been the only things allowed originally, but "ropes" had come to include nets, and "sticks" a number of ingenious wooden implements for holding or herding. We practiced hobbling, netting and herding on the bulls at Ph'stos. But, of course, no bull kept in close pasture was really wild, and we had to catch our bull out on the open ranges. It was desirable to catch a bull as early as possible in the season, it gave you that much more time to train it. So we awaited anxiously reports from road guards and herdsmen about the state and the readiness of the bulls. Domestic bulls are apparently differently disposed, but the wild bulls on the hills have a regular rutting season like stags. It was important that the roads be open by the time this started so we could get our decoy cow up there; it was too chancy to count on catching a wild cow for a decoy.

But now disturbing reports began to come down from the herdsmen. A great white bull had been seen among the herds, driving off the other bulls from the cows and fighting with those who would not be driven off. For a really new bull, one not seen before by the herdsmen, to be found among the flocks was a portent in itself and this bull was acting in an unnatural way. An ordinary bull is content with its own bit of range and as many cows as it could serve and keep together. But this bull was wandering over the whole range and scaring off or attacking other bulls without building up a harem of its own.

The herdsmen told us that such a bull had been observed years before. Rough calculations from what they told us gave us a time around the time Astariano must have been conceived, and none of us had failed to make an immediate connection between a white bull and the story about Astariano's birth. Even an ordinary rogue bull would be a problem in catching a bull for the Dance, and a supernatural bull would pose unpredictable dangers. I still refused to believe that any god would want to turn himself into a real bull, even one of the Gods Below. But if I could control a bull, a god should have no trouble doing so, and a bull under the control of a hostile god would be as great a danger to us as a god in bull form.

But there was no chance for me to go up to the hills and reconnoiter; by the time we had heard the news it was time to make our way into the range where the bulls roamed. We camped in the hills the first night out and heard strange bellowings in the dark. Even the decoy cow, a fine sleek creature, was sweating and trembling by the time the night was over, and my Dancers and I got little sleep.

None of our friends could go with us or help us in any way until we had caught the bull, so there were only our original fourteen from Athens. The girls except for Alceme were more a liability than a help and besides Glaukos and Menesthius there were only two or three of the boys I really trusted in a pinch. In the morning when we broke our fast and tied the decoy cow to a tree, I had a grim feeling that we four Leapers would be just as well off, and perhaps better, if we had come alone.

At first it looked as if things would be easy. A fine-looking, young dappled bull came trotting up the valley sniffing the air and curveting a little in the early spring sun. He was somewhat young, but looked good-tempered and intelligent. He sniffed the cow and came trotting eageriy over in our direction. But suddenly from the hills above there was an ear-splitting bellow and a great white bull came charging down like an avalanche. I had just been able to touch the young bull's mind from a distance and feel something of his joy and strength, but trying to reach the mind of this one gave the same prickly stinging sensation as the seal long ago in Daedalus's workshop.

I could see the next moves taking place in my mind as inevitable as the choreographed moves in a Dance. The young bull and any other bulls attracted by the cow would be killed or driven away. The white bull would either kill us here or allow himself to be captured and kill us in the Dance. Certainly, I could no more control that creature than I could the avalanche it resembled.

I made up my mind to break the pattern. Whispering to Alceme, "Look after things here," I broke cover and ran straight across the white bull's path. With a roar he was after me, following me across the broken ground I had headed for and gaining on me steadily. When I swung into a low tree he headed for it with another roar. He seemed quite capable of knocking down the tree and trampling it and me to pieces.

But all I had wanted was to get the bull away from the others and out of their sight. As soon as I was in the tree my hand went to my hair and the gryphon feather was floating in the air. Again as before there was the golden flash and the great gryphon hovered before me as his feather returned to my hand for the last time. I pointed at the white bull who had stopped at the flash and when he saw what had appeared started racing away even faster than he had charged.

"Can you get rid of it?" I called, pointing to the bull.

"Yes," came the calm, remote voice. "Farewell."

It was never really a contest, but it was thrilling nevertheless. The bull raced frantically away, every muscle straining, but with a few beats of its wings the gryphon gained altitude and overtook it. Then the wings folded and the gryphon swooped on the bull as a hawk does on a rabbit. The balled claws hit the bull behind the neck and it rolled over and went limp. The gryphon settled on it and grasped it with claws and paws, then the wings beat as if they would shake the earth with their force and the gryphon and its victim rose slowly into the air. As the gryphon mounted there was a struggle from the bull and just before the familiar golden flash it seemed to me that perhaps the bull no longer looked like a bull. But whatever it was the gryphon held it and after the flash both gryphon and demonic bull were gone as if they had never been.

I returned to the tree to find all of the Athenians laughing and shouting and dancing, even the more timid girls. When I had led the white bull away, the young dappled bull had trotted over to the cow and got to work so busily that he had been hobbled, roped and netted before he realized what had happened. It was standing there, netted and held with ropes staked to the ground bellowing with surprise and outrage. No one had been hurt and even the bull was more insulted than really angry. In fact, his outraged bellows were so funny that he was immediately dubbed "Baby," and though he was later given a more resounding name, I do not recall that any of us ever used it.

Chapter Twelve: ATHENS

We thought once again that our troubles were over. Whoever was responsible for the white bull—and we suspected M'nos and Astariano in combination—had tried to alter the one element of the Dance not in our control. With a good bull—and Baby, despite his youth, was shaping well—and well-trained Leapers and an experienced tauromath, it was hard to see what could happen to us in the Dance. This time it was Menesthius who brought us back to earth. "Even supposing we're right," he said, "and that M'nos can find no further way to attack us—I don't really believe that, but let it go for the moment—but what about the next group of Athenians?"

We looked at him, dumbfounded. We had been worrying about ourselves, forgetting that M'nos had plans to make the substitution of Athenians for "the children of M'nos" a permanent change. But once the question was raised the problems were obvious. Menesthius stated some of them. "What's the chance that there will be anyone in the group who can be a tauromath? How likely is it that even two girls out of the seven will be willing or able to be Leapers? Suppose M'nos simply lets us have our year and then has his revenge on us and on Athens by doing to them what he had planned to do to us? How would we feel as their trainers?"

The six of us were talking together at Ph'stos where we had brought the bull after his capture. Our excuse was that the roads were still too bad to move from Ph'stos, but actually it would have been almost as easy to take the bull directly to N'sos. We hoped that by delaying our return we could delay M'nos's getting to know that we had disposed of the white bull and gotten an ordinary trainable bull in its stead. For all our brave talk about there being nothing more M'nos could do to us, probably deep down all of us expected some new stroke from him.

Ariadne spoke, breaking the gloomy silence. "I hate to make things worse, but I don't think that we can count on sending anyone through the Path to find a vision for a seal to strengthen their powers as tauromath. Until I'm very sure Astariano is out of the way permanently, I wouldn't risk anyone on the Path. I was persuaded to do it for Chryseis because there was no other way, and because I had good reason to believe that she had some unusual powers. But to send a person with no extraordinary powers except an empathy with animals might only open us to another attack from M'nos. Astariano has some kind of power over the Path. I don't believe he was ever lost in it at all. He was lurking in it and when it suited him to come out and join M'nos he did."

Silence settled over us again and finally Alceme spoke. "There's only one solution. Someone knowledgeable must go to Athens and select the right people for the next group of Dancers." We all brightened, but then as the difficulties struck us slumped into dejection again.

"M'nos would never let me go," said Ariadne. "And as for giving permission to one of you... I don't know. Much as I hate to say it, we could make the best case for Chryseis. The Mistress of the Dance has traditionally had the privilege of choosing who is to be a novice, if there's any question of eligibility. In one way M'nos would probably be glad to have Chryseis out of Kaphtu; it's largely due to her that he's been defeated so far. But I don't know..."

"But how would I know whom to choose?" I burst out. "And when would I have time to go. And..."

Riatano, who had been in charge of arrangements spoke up. "The first Dance this year is at the Ship Festival, when the sea is declared safe for sailing. No ship will go to Athens before that. And the next Dance isn't held until the first ship returns from a mainland port—little trips to the Circle Islands don't count. So Chryseis could go after the first Dance and be back for the second."

Now Alceme spoke up. "I know all of the girls on the Hill, remember I was a palace brat. Before we all decided to be 'grown up' some of us were pretty fair hellions. I remember some games we played on the palace guards... Well never mind. But there are a few girls that I'd trust with a bull and luckily most of them will still be virgins, because Aegeus doesn't want marriages between families he doesn't trust—it might strengthen ties against him—and he trusts very few people."

I nodded, "Girls will be the problem, of course. Between Menesthius and Glaukos I can get a list of boys with courage and good sense; we'll have to depend on two having that something extra that makes a Leaper. But that still leaves..."

Menesthius spoke up. "A tauromath. I've been wondering about that. Does the tauromath have to be a girl?"

Ariadne shook her head. "No and neither does the Leader of the Dance have to be a girl. My brother was tauromath and Master of the Dance in his year. It's even possible for tauromath and Leader to be different people, though that's not usually wise. Do you know someone who might be able to do it, Menesthius?"

He nodded slowly. "I've been wondering about it ever since this problem occurred to me. There's a cousin of mine whose mother was a priestess of Artemis, Mistress of Wild Things. They usually stay virgin, you know, but my cousin's father was a younger brother of King Pandion and the temple was persuaded to let my cousin's mother go. I suppose she was willing, otherwise even Pandion couldn't have managed it. But she would wander off into the wilds occasionally taking Artimodorous—that's my cousin—with her. Whether by training or inheritance he got a power over animals I've never seen equaled until Chryseis got her new seal. But since he has that power already..."

"He wouldn't have to walk the Path!" burst out Ariadne. "So all of our problems would be solved." She looked consideringly at Alceme and Menesthius. "You two have been figuring this out between you.

144

This comes too pat for it to be just on the spur of the moment."

Alceme and Menesthius grinned at each other.

"Glaukos too," said Alceme. "And we consulted Riatano on some things. You two needn't think you have a monopoly on doing things. We're part of the group, too."

Menesthius spoke up, fearing with his usual considerateness that our feelings might be hurt. "It isn't that we don't appreciate all that you and Chryseis have done for us, Ariadne. But we wanted to pull our weight, too."

"You have," said Aridane. "You've not only recognized the problem, you've largely solved it. Chryseis and I have been reacting too much to M'nos, waiting for his next move. You've looked ahead. There are still problems, though. What was the process by which you were chosen?"

I let Menesthius answer. I was feeling an almost maternal pride in him and Alceme and was eager to encourage their independence.

"There was a form of casting lots," said Menesthius. "But everyone knows old Calchis is a creature of Aegeus's. There wasn't much doubt that Aegeus chose who was to go or at least exempted any of his favorites' children."

"So, M'nos will have to send messages demanding that a representative of Kaphtu choose the fourteen," said Ariadne. "That and persuading him to let Chryseis go at all will be our biggest problem."

But in the end things proved unexpectedly easy. We returned to N'sos reluctantly when we could no longer use the roads as an excuse, but we found that no one had seen Astariano since the day the gryphon had taken the white bull, and that M'nos was sunk in some sort of depression and was under the treatment by the best Healers of the court. I still refused to believe that either Astariano or whatever being was his father had been the white bull. But that Astariano or M'nos or both had been controlling the white bull in some way I could easily believe. If a bull were killed while under my control I could imagine it doing terrible things to me; perhaps that was what had happened to M'nos.

I resolutely turned my mind away from that last glimpse of the bull twisting and seeming to change its shape. If it was some sort of demon I was sure that Gyros, the gryphon, was more than a match for it. I felt that when I had to use the feather for the last time and lost the ability to summon Gyros to my aid, I would be very naked and exposed to my enemies. Not only that, the creature itself fascinated me; I felt that I would like to get to know it better than it seemed likely that I ever would.

Because of the incapacity of M'nos, Ariadne was able simply to take charge. She made arrangements for me to go on the ship that would go to Athens to fetch the next group of seven boys and seven girls for the Dance, and ordered that the ship be the first to leave after the Ship Festival. A major disappointment was that we could not have P'sero's ship, but he was already deeply involved in a trading venture to Egypt. He offered to cancel his arrangements, but this would have meant letting down partners who depended on him and we refused reluctantly. In the end, we settled on a friend of P'sero's—an experienced older captain who had held the Purple Oar several times. We had one close friend in the crew, Kom'ku, who had been Ariadne's partner in the Dance, was now apprentice to the captain we chose, whose name was N'mirano.

I had missed P'sero and his family while we were across the island in Ph'stos with the roads across the mountains often closed. N'suto had visited us a few times; he had fallen victim to Alceme's charms. She treated him with a sort of amiable contempt that he put up with humbly. He had probably never been much interested in girls, being so sea-mad, but Alceme had made a sudden and deep impression. To my surprise P'sero did not disapprove.

"If she'll have him, he could do much worse," he said. "A seaman needs a wife with courage and independence, and she has both. She'll come dowered with her jewels, and with more than that if this trading venture goes well. My son will be a wealthy man when I die and I can set him up well when he marries."

It seemed a coldish basis for a marriage, but N'suto was certainly infatuated with Alceme and she seemed as fond of him as she was of anyone. I looked at P'sero affectionately. "I almost wish…" I said, and he knew what I meant.

"I'd like well to have you as a daughter, my dear," he said. "But though N'suto is my son and plenty good enough for Alceme, I wouldn't choose him for you. In fact, I don't know a man whom I would. Or for Ariadne either and that's a problem for the whole realm. Marry she must, and give us a king, but whom will she find that will he a fit match for her and a good sailor-king?"

I knew no more than he did, but was less inclined to worry; even if M'nos died it would not hurt Kaphtu to be ruled by a woman till she found a husband to suit her.

One thing I did on my visits to P'sero, which were as frequent as I could make them, was to stop in the fishermen's quarter to visit the baby whom I had helped in the cave of Eluethia while he was still in his mother's womb. Riamare, P'sero's wife, was still not as close a friend as I wished, but I was working on her reserve and she located the mother and baby for me easily enough and without awkward questions, when I asked her to. It was easy enough to find an excuse to pass by the house, and to admire the baby. After that I was welcomed whenever I passed by. The mother was younger than she had looked in the cave and this was her first child. The father was a young fisherman.

I had been haunted by Dion's words, "It may be born an idiot or deformed," and I was pleased to see that it was a fat, healthy child, who seemed to my inexperience vastly clever for its age. They had named it Anadamano, though names beginning with the "A" sound were usually reserved for royal children. The priestess had allowed the naming because of the mother's story, borne out by the change in her condition, of being helped by a "goddess." To my relief she showed no signs of recognizing me. But I was always welcome in the house and enjoyed visiting there. Babies are fascinating creatures and the simple life in the little fisherman's house was much more what I had grown up with than the life of the palace.

Practice, of course, took up most of my time. We would have three Leapers who could do a head leap, which would be spectacular enough to make up for the lesser number of Leapers from last year. But the smaller number was harder to choreograph: Baby had to make two runs back and forth to give us a chance. Baby seemed to me to be so easy to handle that I felt that Alceme or Menesthius or even Glaukos might be able to get some rapport with him if I helped. But except for some very feeble results with Menesthius it was no use. Baby would not hurt any of us intentionally, I believed, but he didn't know his strength, and certainly without me he could not be guided through the Dance.

Our first Dance of the year went well, with M'nos huddled in his throne with unseeing eyes, but all other eyes seemingly friendly. The novelty of Athenian Dancers had worn off last year. and we were regarded merely as Dancers. I still got calls of "Atane" when the crowd was pleased. I was amused to find that Alceme had gotten the nickname "Phane," which means "golden lady" and is very much the same name as "Chryseis" in Danaan. The three head leaps went well; we did them in sequence at the end of the Dance after each doing one on the three previous runs.

I sometimes wished I could see the Dance from the crowd. The triple head leap must have been quite beautiful to see. As one of the Leapers I had barely landed from my own leap before I had to turn and steady Menesthius coming over after me; he then wheeled and touched Alceme's hands as she came over. And of course I was busy slowing Baby as soon as Alceme was in the air coming off of his back. By this time he was almost at the south wall and I had to slow him enough to negotiate the turn into the corridor where the handlers took over. Ariadne, who could handle Baby through her link with me as I had been able to handle Winey through my link with her, did the leap several times with Menesthius and Alceme on the practice field so that I could judge the effect and figure distance and speed. But that was not quite the same as seeing it in the Dance itself in the setting of the Great Court.

If I had not had the trip to Athens to look forward to I would probably have felt quite let down during the gap between the Ship Festival and the Festival of Return. The ordinary group of Dancers uses this interval to correct the mistakes they have made in their first Dance and tighten up their choreography, but Glaukos, Alceme, Menesthius and I had worked together for so much of the previous season that we had made no special mistakes and needed little revision in the Dance we had choreographed. Of course, you must always improve, but there is a difference between correcting and improving. We could improve and did, but needed no corrections.

We directed our ingenuity instead to "choreographing" my trip to Athens. We agreed early on that it would not do for me to appear as myself, Chryseis the Athenian; it would raise too many questions. So it was settled that I was to be the mysterious Kaphtui priestess who had been sent by

M'nos to select the next group. Real Kaphtui dress would be shocking to Athenian eyes, so Ariadne, Alceme and I devised a modified version of a Kaphtui woman's dress, with less elaborate flounces and a jacket which closed in front. Something rather similar was becoming fashionable among the court ladies of the Danaan kingdoms in Argos and it would look sufficiently "Cretan" to the Athenians.

We had determined that I must be disguised as an older woman, both to conceal my identity and to give me more authority. Alceme knew a woman very skilled in face painting, who was able to reverse her usual skill for making older women look young to make me look older. But I was not satisfied that the result would be convincing in bright sunlight, and in the end we got some very fine Egyptian material, an almost transparent linen, and dyed it a dark blue, almost black. The effect was very similar to the way Ariadne looked to my eyes when she wore the Veil of Adis. I could see out well enough, but the dark veil over my face and body made my "old woman" paint completely convincing as well as shrouding me in mystery.

We had originally thought of asking Daedalus to make us some sort of lot-casting device which could be manipulated by the holder but which looked completely fair. But he suggested a more effective idea.

"I'm sorry to refuse the challenge," he said. "It would be amusing to design something of the sort. But no matter how well I made it Athenians would suspect Cretan trickery. Use a house snake instead. You can control it easily with your seal, but no one will suspect you of being able to manipulate it." This was such a good idea that it was immediately adopted and elaborated.

So everything was ready after the Festival of Ships and at the first light of dawn the next morning, I embraced my friends and boarded N'miriano's ship. The next days were a repetition of the voyage to Kaphtui although we rowed more and sailed less. As an honored passenger I took my seat with the officers as a matter of course and the ship waited for me to have a good swim in the mornings. This was not just self-indulgence; it was essential that I return in good shape for the Dance which would follow our return.

I wore my Dancer's kilt and enjoyed the sun and wind on my body, becoming quite unfashionably tanned. Even Ariadne and Alceme shielded themselves from the sun as much as they could, and an ordinary court lady would go to great lengths to keep her skin from the slightest touch of sun. If I enjoyed the voyage less than my first one, it was only because of the absence of P'sero. It looked strange to look at the captain's chair and not see him. But Kom'ku, who had been a Dancer, was good company and I enjoyed roaming the ship and chatting with the sailors. All sailors love to tell tales, true and false, about their voyages and now that I really understood Kaphtui, as I had not on my previous voyage, I loved to listen to their tales.

When we first landed at Phaleron and took the familiar road to Athens I felt a great sense of homecoming. Athens seemed the greatest city in the world and I felt a homesickness for it that I had been too busy to feel while I was away. But something about Phaleron and then about Athens itself bothered me and I realized it was the women. There were very few on the streets and those who were out on business of one kind or another were subdued and submissive, a striking contrast to the vivid women of Kaphtu. It was then, I think, that I really decided that my future was in Kaphtu. Athens was a great city, but not for women, at least women like myself.

The Choosing itself went much as we had planned it. The "youths and maidens," past childhood but still unmarried, were assembled for us on the Hill in front of Athena's temple. I asked that the temple snake be brought out to me, giving the priestess a sign that Ariadne had obtained from the priestess of Atana in Kaphtu. When she obeyed, I went down the lines of boys and girls asking each to say their names. When I recognized a name that Alceme, Glaukos, or Menesthius had given me I matched it to a carefully memorized description and then tried to make a snap judgment of suitability. A few faces were too sullen or untrustworthy and I was pretty sure that one young "virgin" was pregnant, but in most cases my judgment matched that of my friends. When I chose someone I made the snake reach out and touch them with his head, otherwise it stayed coiled around my shoulders and arm. The arm ached with its weight before I was through. It was a very old snake and very large and heavy. It had probably not had so much exercise in years.

When I came to Artimodorous, I knew that he would realize that I was controlling the snake, and I wondered what he would do. To my surprise he drew the snake toward him with his own powers before I had a chance to make it touch him; he was evidently eager to go. I let him do it, but took back control of the snake after it had touched him, to let him know I could do it. His eyes widened as I did so: he probably thought I had a natural power over animals like his own. I smiled and nodded at him, trying to let him see I approved and wished him well.

The fourteen were soon chosen and since everyone but Artimodorus thought that they had been chosen by Athena's snake, there were no complaints and no murmuring against the choices. Aegeus had not been pleased when N'miriano, as ambassador of M'nos, had told him that we would choose the fourteen, but since we had no desire to take away any of his pampered favorites, he was satisfied in the end. He was a foxy-looking man which is not always the case with men who have foxy minds. I could see traces of red in his gray hair and there was a very slight resemblance to my father. But Aegeus's expression was hard and suspicious, and that of a ruler who trusts no one. I was glad my father had chosen to be a craftsman.

As soon as the fourteen were chosen they were marched off to the ship, but I had the herald announce that their families could bring clothing and possessions to the ship and say farewells there. I had plans of my own for the few hours that would take. When we were in a narrow lane coming down from the hill I dropped behind, slipped off my veil of dyed Egyptian stuff and covered myself with an old cloak I had borrowed from Alceme. I was now just an old Athenian woman, if you did not look at me too closely and I made my way around the hill and down heart-rendingly familiar lanes to a house I knew very well.

The door was open, as it was most days, and my father was not alone. A servant girl from some wealthy merchant's house had brought a piece of work and like most servant girls she was more eager to idle in the craftsman's workshop than to get back to her duties. How could I get rid of her? I decided to pretend to be my mother's foster mother, Phiane, who had once or twice visited us in Athens.

"Well, son-in-law," I said in a voice as much like hers as I could manage, "I've a little time in Athens on temple business, so I've come to see you."

As my father looked up a series of expressions crossed his face. First astonishment with a touch of fear, then for a second an incredulous joy, then recognition and a tenderer, calmer joy. I was to understand the first expression shortly; the second I realized meant that he had thought for a moment that I was my mother returned to him. He rose to his feet, bustled the servant girl out of the door and closed it, then came and embraced me in a bear hug. Setting me on my feet again he regarded me with a familiar teasing smile, though there were tears in his eyes.

"A little hasty as usual, daughter. Poor Phiane died last winter and some people in the neighborhood know it. When that little minx wags her tongue I'll be a portent—a man visited by the ghost of his mother-in-law."

Blinking back my own tears, I smiled at him affectionately. "Never mind that now, you'll think of some story. I can't stay long, father, the ship I came on has to be out of port tonight, because of the fourteen. But let me wash this stuff off my face, though I'll have to put it on again. I want you to really see me." And getting a pitcher of water from the big vase I went with a slightly unsteady step into my own little room to wash my face.

Chapter Thirteen: THE PIRATES

A little later my father and I were sitting at our table, eating (what else?) bread and olives, and drinking resinated wine. The story of my year in Kaphtu had been poured out and we were now chatting quietly together as we had always done about things that interested us.

"Daedalus is quite right," said my father. "M'nos is a good hater, as you know. He hates Rhadamantes and he hates me because I was Rhadamantes's friend. So, much as I'd like to, I can't come back with you. But now that I know you're safe I may leave Athens. Living here without your mother and without you is too full of memories. I may even join old fire-head Rhadamantes in his little kingdom on the coasts of Asia. I'll get words to you; Cretan ships go everywhere."

I looked at him earnestly, "Father, about Mother. Daedalus knew something, but wouldn't tell. Can you tell me now? Did she have something to do with the Bright Land?"

He smiled affectionately. "I'm glad Daedalus didn't tell you; it's my privilege. Yes, it's time to tell you, daughter. We always said that your mother served the temple of Aphaea on Aegina. We let you think she was a priestess there. But the truth is..." He smiled ruefully and looked into my eyes. "Your mother 'served' the temple as its goddess. You are Britomartis, daughter of Britomartis, Aphaea daughter of Aphaea. Your mother is the goddess of Aegina."

I goggled at him and he kept on talking, partly to let me recover but partly because memories which he had never been able to speak of were crowding in. "I went there as a wild young devil, fresh from knocking around with Daedalus and Rhadamantes all over Crete and the Islands, and Asia. I stopped on Aegina on my way home. The high priestess asked me to do a carving of the goddess. I said jokingly that if I could see the goddess, I could do a better piece of work. To my astonishment she agreed. If I spent the night in the temple, the goddess would appear to me. I did; she did. You remember your mother, how beautiful, how sweet she was. I lost my head and kissed her. If she had blasted me I would have died happy. But she kissed me back."

He paused and went on. "By some miracle she loved me as I loved her, at first sight. We were determined to be together, to have children. She left Aegina and came to Athens as my wife. Every summer she returned to do what she could for her temple and her people there. You know how much time she spent at the temple during our summers there. But she could stay with us no longer than eight years. It was the condition on which the Olympians allowed her to marry a mortal. Then she had to return to Olympus— what you call the Bright Land—for eight years, not come to this world at all. Those eight years are nearly

up. We may very well see her again; we will if she has
the choice, if they let her. But I don't think they'll ever
let her live here again, as she did for those eight years."

It was too much to take in all at once. I seized on
the least personal element of the story. "What is
Olympus—the Bright Land? How is it connected to
our world?" I asked.

My father nodded. "I've pondered that myself. I
think its a whole world, a cosmos, separated from ours,
but somehow near it." He pointed to two pots near the
hearth. "They paint figures on pots sometimes,
especially in Crete. Suppose those figures were alive,
but flat. They could only move around on the surface
of the pot; that would be their whole world. But what if
the pots were touching. Perhaps a figure could wander
from one pot to the other. If the pot nearer the fire was
hot, the figure might carry the heat with it. It could use
that heat to warm or burn figures on the pot it went to.
That's what the Olympians do: carry power from their
world to ours."

"I see," I cried. "But are they just men and women
like us then, but with more power?"

He shook his head. "I've left out one thing in my
little story. The creatures that lived on the hotter pot
might be different from those on the cooler pot. But if
they could interbreed their descendants would have
characteristics of both 'races.' That's what the
Olympians are; part human and part—something else.
The Old Gods, the Titans, lived in that world before
humans came there. Rhea was one of them. The poets
and priests say Cronos was too. But that's wrong.
Cronos was a human being who wandered into the

Bright Land. The children of Cronos and Rhea are the Three Kings—Zeus, Poseidon, and Hades—and the Three Queens—Hestia, Demeter, and Hera. The other Olympians are all children of Zeus by Hera or by one of the Titanesses, except Hephaestus. He's Hera's revenge: her child by a Titan, not a son of Zeus."

"But how could Titans and humans interbreed if they're different species?" I asked. "You used to say…"

He interrupted. "I know. But the Titans apparently can take any form they like. If they take human form, it's a human form which is real enough to interbreed with humans. But they don't always take human form. Your friend, Gyros the gryphon, is almost certainly a Titan."

I nodded slowly. "The Land itself—it's like an imitation of this world."

He looked at me. "Yes. The Titans formed not only themselves but their world according to the images they found in Cronos's mind. Why they did, not even the Olympians know. But that's why their world is so like ours."

I approached the personal element now. "And Mother…"

He smiled tenderly. "Your mother is the daughter of Zeus by Metis, one of the Titanesses. Athena is her sister. But Athena is hardly human at all, at least from what I've seen of her.' And your mother is all human. The relation of children to parents is strange. My father Pandion didn't have red hair, but his father did. Aegeus and I were both red-headed, but our brother, Pallas, wasn't. Somehow Cronos's humanity came down to some of the Olympians and not others. Hera is 'human' in one sense: petty, spiteful, vindictive. Poseidon is as inhuman as the sea he rules. You have some idea: you saw him. The less human Olympians treat humans almost like playthings. The more human ones pity us and try to help us, as your mother did. She took one good-sized island, Aegina, and did what she could to make it peaceful and happy."

One question out of the many in my mind, came to my lips. "What about—" I lowered my voice— "Those Below?" My father's face was grim. "They're real enough, and bad enough. Most of them are Titans, too. There was a sort of war between two factions of them when Cronos entered their world. Cronos allied himself with the side that was, if not exactly friends of humans, at least well disposed to us. But the other side is clever; they eventually got to Cronos and he went over to their side. He tried to destroy his children, but Rhea was too clever for him. When Zeus grew up he allied himself with the friendly Titans to defeat Cronos and the malevolent Titans. Somehow Zeus and his allies were able to hurl their enemies out of Olympus; not to our world but to a world of even less power: the Dark World."

He looked down at his hands, a habit of his when he was thinking deeply. "They say the Dark World is the world of the Dead. I don't know about that. But it's the prison of Cronos and the defeated Titans and they can't get out of it. Nor can Hades, the Third King. He's their jailer but he can't return to Olympus either. No Olympian who goes to the Dark World can return to Olympus. And Zeus or the others acting together can hurl a Titan or an Olympian into the Dark World. It's their ultimate threat. If your mother hadn't obeyed them…" His face twisted with pain. "It's the one threat we couldn't face; because it's not certain that I could have joined her even by dying. This way, at least, when she's served her eight years we may be able to see each other sometimes. It's the most we can hope for now."

I shifted uneasily, affected by his pain. "Father, I can't stay much longer. Is there anything more you can tell me that might help me make contact with Mother?"

He nodded slowly. "Crete is the key; that's why I was happy when I knew you'd be going there. I had an idea of what you'd be doing: Rhadamantes had told me about the Dance. And I somehow wasn't surprised that you were chosen. I think that your mother arranged that somehow. She has friends and she uses her mind more than most of the Olympians. You know the Bright Land, as you call it, corresponds to our world. The part of it that corresponds to Crete has some special importance for the Olympians. The story that Rhea concealed Zeus in a cave on Dicte is true. And Dicte itself is some sort of special place. Your mother may even be there, in the mountain in the Bright Land which corresponds to Dicte. But that mountain is defended or guarded somehow. Don't try to go charging up it looking for her."

I had got my bundle from my bedroom and was making up my face as an old woman again. "I have an idea about that," I said, "but I'll be careful. Are you sure you won't take any of the jewels I brought for you?"

He shook his head. "I'll take those things of Daedalus's making you brought me, for the sake of the workmanship. But if I do move I'll travel light. A craftsman can always pay his way by work, and the poorer you are the safer you are when you travel. Speaking of safety, watch out for Dion if you meet him again. Something about him bothers me. He told you his mother was Semele. I think Zeus had a son by a Theban woman of that name, and I have a feeling that I've heard something worrying about that son. But watch out for any Olympian. Sometimes they don't know their own power, or think of what will happen if they use it."

I was finished now, and couldn't keep the ship waiting any longer. My father and I clung to each other for a moment. Despite our confident plans we might not see each other again. Then I draped the cloak around me, picked up my little bundle and left the house behind, heading for Phaleron. I hurried along the road as fast as I could without belying my disguise as an old woman. I could have saved my breath. When I got to the harbor there was not a sight of the Kaphtui ship. It had sailed, leaving me stranded on the mainland.

I almost turned back to my father. But the weight of responsibiity was on my shoulders; my Dancers needed me back. I went down to the docks to see if I could find out anything. My heart leaped as I saw the figure of Kom'ku slumped on the edge of the dock. He leaped up and embraced me, causing curious glances from the dock loungers. He burst into speech: since I was sure none of those on the dock spoke Kaphtui I let him talk.

"I told N'miriano that he should wait a little longer, that you wouldn't keep us waiting long. But he insisted on obeying the orders exactly. They said to wait for nothing. Chryseis, the great fire mountain on Dariapana is throwing fire and ash into the air; burying the fields and towns. Every Kaphtui ship is ordered to take people off before the mountain kills them."

I thought frantically. Dariapana was the nearest of the Circle Islands to Kaphtu and was an important Kaphtui colony—the only case where the Kaphtui had taken over a whole island instead of just establishing a trading post or small settlement. It was a place where many young Kaphtui went to find more freedom and more opportunities than they could in the more settled life of Kaphtu itself. People called it New Kaphtu, or Katu—the Beautiful Island. P'sero had a married younger sister there. Probably N'miriano had relations there; many seamen did. It probably explained why he had not stayed for me.

"Did you stay behind just to let me know?" I asked.

He smiled a little sheepishiy. "Not really, Chryseis. I did fight to be the one who would stay, but someone had to be left here to try to find Athenian ships to help evacuate the island. But I've failed. Not one of the captains will do it. They claim that Aegeus wouldn't allow it, and they don't like Kaphtu anyway because of the war and the Tribute." That was understandable but frustrating. I was beginning to worry about those people on Dariapana.

Kom'ku was looking to me for orders: for half a year I had been Mistress of the Dance and he one of my Dancers. Luckily, I had some orders I could give. "All right, come with me. I know the captain of a fishing boat that used to take my father and me to Aegina. He'll take you there for me. The men of Aegina are fine seamen and not under Aegeus's thumb. You can probably persuade them to help by promises of rewards from M'nos, if they won't help just because help is needed. But I think they will; they're good people. If you have any trouble go to the temple of Aphaea. Tell the high priestess..." I paused. "Tell her that Chryseis daughter of Chryseis of the temple who married Lykos the Athenian sent you and asked her to help you."

We walked to where I knew the fishing boats from Aegina would be tied up after bringing their catches to the markets of Athens. I told Kom'ku, "I won't come with you now. As an Athenian, I may be able to persuade an Athenian captain to go or at least bribe a foreign trader. I have some jewels me. Every ship may count, and if I have no luck here, I may try another harbor I know of on the Attic coast. If I have no luck at all I'll get to Aegina and come on an Aeginan boat. They won't all be ready to leave at once."

Luckily I found one of my friends in the Aeginan fishing fleet quickly, a man who remembered me as the little girl who did not get seasick and whose mother was someone important at the Temple. He agreed to take Kom'ku immediately and I said my farewells on the shore where the fishing boats were drawn up.

Kom'ku hugged me and said, "Don't worry about the Dance, Chryseis. Our ships won't make port in Kaphtu. Small boats will intersect our course and tranship the Athenians. The ship will go straight on to Dariapana. So there'll be no Homecoming Festival for awhile, even if they were mad enough to have a Festival while this is going on."

I was considerably cheered by this as I went back to the harbor where the bigger seagoing boats lay. The relentless pressure of time had eased. My problem now was as many ships as I could get for the evacuation of Dariapana. But this proved harder than I thought. I had washed my makeup off for the Aeginans and put it on again to disguise my youth. But I spoke to the ships' captains as an Athenian. Most of them were not only uncooperative but surly—why should I or they or any Athenian worry about Kaphtui? Let their mountain fall on them and kill them all. But some of this surliness, I think, came from shame. Their ordinary instinct would have been to help but they knew Aegeus would not let them.

Finally, I was forced to settle for a single merchant ship, an island trader. I distrusted the captain, whose eyes had gleamed a little too brightly at the sight of my jewels, but his words were plausible: "Lady, I am taking a party to Naxos for some kind of religious celebration. As soon as I drop them I will take you to Dariapana to do whatever you wish. You may find at least one other ship in harbor at Naxos, perhaps more. It's no use asking at other Attic harbors—Aegeus has given orders about helping the Kaphtui in any way."

Against my better judgment, I gave in. Even if he was dishonest, a party of pilgrims would be some protection and Naxos was much nearer Kaphtu than Phaleron. When I saw that the party of pilgrims were all women it was too late to cry off. The gangplank came aboard as soon as the last pilgrim was boarded, and the men pushed off with their oars; we were under way.

It was already late; we just made Sunion by dark. I had half hoped to see N'miriano's ship there, but they were probably sailing night and day. They had taken the small swift messenger ship which had delivered their orders in tow. Oarsmen from the ship would nearly double their available oarsmen and they could row in shifts late into the night if the wind did not serve. I lay down with the pilgrim women that night feeling I had done all I could.

In the morning we set sail early and I was happy to be at sea again. But presently I sensed something wrong. I checked the sun and the land falling away behind us and then faced the captain. "We aren't going to Naxos," I said loudly enough for the other passengers to hear. "We're going north along the coast, toward the Pirate Islands." As soon as the words were out of my mouth my heart sank. I realized that there was a very simple explanation for that. The captain looked at me, pulling his beard and smiling a nasty smile and I knew I was right: this was a pirate ship which had slipped into Phaleron disguised as a trader.

"Things would have been more pleasant—for awhile—if you had kept your mouth shut," he sneered. "But since you know, we might as well see what kind of merchandise we have for the slave market. Strip them down," he bawled to his crew. "Let's see what we've got."

I put my hand on my belt knife, but he ignored me for the moment. There were shrieks from the pilgrim women and a disgusted crewman shouted to the captain' "Old women some of them. Might as well throw them overboard. Hey! This one's a boy in women's clothing!" He hauled a figure up to the captain and with a shock of surprise I saw a familiar face. Dion! Looking cool and somewhat amused, half in and half out of his woman's robe.

"Am I to understand that you are not taking my friends and me to Naxos?" he asked insolently. His eyes flickered over me and he grinned.

The captain's sneer grew uglier. "We have other plans for you, my pretty boy. Like to dress up as a woman, do you? Well, some of my men have strange tastes. Perhaps I'll give you to them to play with."

The old steersman, whose face might have been a noble one before too much wine had destroyed it, protested feebly. "Captain, no! You'll offend the gods!"

The captain knocked down the old man with a swipe from the back of his hand and turned toward Dion again.

But Dion held his eyes and began speaking in deep, hypnotic tones. "To play with, eh, captain? You like to play perhaps, to sing and dance and drink?" He picked up a bunch of grapes that the captain had been nibbling and squeezed them between his fingers. "Wine from grapes," he almost chanted. "But you need more grapes. Grapes from vines." I could see tendrils of grape vine coming from his fingers. He threw the bunch of grapes at the foot of the mast and gestured at them. The tendrils wound around the mast. I could see a few small leaves.

But from the goggle-eyed stares of the captain and crew they saw much more. From the direction of their looks I guessed what they saw. Vines, great heavy vines laden with grapes winding up the mast and along the yard, crawling along the deck—I saw them move their feet to avoid illusory vines I could not see. Vines winding around the stempost and over the captain's chair, crawling over their bodies and pinning their arms to their sides. I could see them struggling against the illusory bonds, their arms unable to leave their sides.

Dion spoke again. "Someone spoke of going overboard. A nice day for a swim. Especially if you're a dolphin. And you are dolphins, all of you!" His voice was raised to a shout and I saw the captain and crew hop grotesquely to the rail, imagining their feet changed to flukes, their arms to fins, their faces to dolphins' beaks. As I watched horror-stricken they leaped overboard. One or two of them even bobbed to the surface once or twice, trying to imitate dolphins' leaps. Then they disappeared under the waves.

Dion stepped toward the old steersman who had been saved by being only half-conscious after the captain's blow. I raised my hand in front of him. He stopped and looked at me with eyes that had a sort of madness in them. A little flame seemed to flicker over his head, the same color as the flash of light that had accompanied the gryphon's appearances. I tried to speak calmly. "The old man spoke up for you. And you won't get to Naxos without a steersman." He nodded. "Let him live. He can join my worshipers. But you won't, will you, Britomartis? I'm sorry you can't have this ship, my dear. I need it."

He paused for a moment and I could hear the women shouting ecstatically, their feet pounding the deck in a sort of dance. "Io, Io Dionysus," they screamed.

The madness returned to his eyes and the flame flared brighter. "I'll give you a lift, however, Britomartis. Go with my blessings!"

I felt a sort of tremendous blow on my body; golden light flared in my eyes. Then I was falling, tumbling down to end with a splash in the sea. I shook the hair out of my eyes and began to swim. Above me was the sun of the Bright Land. Around me the sea was empty: the ship had vanished. My father's words rang in my mind, "Don't trust Dion... a son of Zeus... something worrying about him..., the Olympians don't know their own strength."

Chapter Fourteen:THE FIRE-MOUNTAIN

The sea was not as cold as I expected, and for awhile I floated there, trying to look around me. There were no islands that I could see, though you can see surprisingly little when you are immersed in the sea, and the mainland was only a faint loom far away. I could not imagine dying in this land, and I felt no fear. But it was hard to see what I could do about my situation. I floated there drawing deep breaths,feeling comfortable and peaceful, waiting. Suddenly something broke water not far from me: a dolphin. Ordinarily, I love dolphins but at the moment the sight of them reminded me of those grotesque figures hopping to the rail. It was regarding me with eyes that seemed intelligent. Could it be... no, nonsense. I forced myself to look into the eye that was toward me, but at this it dived again and was gone.

I floated for a while longer, not apathetic but peaceful; waiting. Then a shadow moved toward the surface from below and there rose out of the water a giant male figure with tangled blue-black beard and hair: Posudi! He lay on his side in the water, as if it were a couch or bed, riding higher in the water than seemed natural. I tried to assume a similar posture, facing him. His sea-green eyes seemed amused, the first human emotion I had seen him display. He spoke as if our meeting in the Central Court had been a few moments ago: "You play a bull well, girl."

I looked at him and decided to throw away caution. "Thank you, Uncle," I said impudently. He laughed a great booming sound with the roar of the sea in it, and, encouraged, I went on. "Is Ariadne your daughter?" I asked. If you want to know you might as well ask: sometimes you get an answer. I did now.

"Yes," said the deep voice casually. "The present M'nos was—unsatisfactory. I—and others—were invited to make up the lack." There was a sly humor in his voice. He might have been any sailor boasting of his conquests.

"She played the bull well, too," I said, wanting to see his reaction.

His face grew sterner. "So she should, being my daughter. If you had not been such an interesting substitute, M'nos would have suffered then. He still may. He has no business using my Dance to get his vengeance. By showing off outside the Dance, Andaroko deserved what he got. Anyway, M'nos has more to worry about now than vengeance."

I suddenly remembered that time was slipping away in my world. "I know. I was trying to get a ship to Dariapana when something happened. Can you get me to Dariapana, greatuncle?" No harm in asking and again I got what I asked for.

"Why not?" He said, booming his great laugh again. "A ride for a ride." His hand touched the water gently, but authoritatively as I might touch a bull in the Dance. A dolphin larger than the one I had seen before, came to the surface near his hand. Posudi's great hand enfolded my arm and half pulled, half lifted me onto the dolphin's back. Once there my body seemed to cling to the dolphin's and I felt I could not fall off if I tried.

The sea-green eyes looked into mine. "You're the first in a long time to stand up on the bull," he said. "I liked that. And your mother is a sweet creature, not like her sister. The seas are kind to her islanders for her sake. They will be kind to you too. Farewell." Suddenly, he sank into the sea again and the dolphin began swimming, staying on the surface as much as it could. Even so the sea dashed in my face and I sometimes gasped for breath. But it was wildly exhilarating—the great body under me, the shining waves slipping past, the wind in my face.

For we were going fast, faster by far than any normal dolphin could swim. I wondered if this was a real dolphin, or whether, like my gryphon, it was something more than it appeared to be. Presently this thought and all thoughts, died from my mind. I was one with the sea and the dolphin. How long it swam I have no idea. A day and a hundred days would have seemed the same to me in my mindless absorplion into the life of the sea. But eventually there was a rocky shore ahead of me and the dolphin slowed and stopped. I slipped from its back as if released and swam into the shore. I lifted one arm to the dolphin; it dived and disappeared.

I had no idea how I could get through into my own world again, but I could not imagine worrying, here in this land. I walked up the shore barefoot and in my kilt.

Richard Purtill

I didn't remember slipping out of the dress I had been
wearing on the ship, but I must have done so sometime
soon after I fell into the sea. Luckily, I wore my kilt
under most other clothing I wore; it was both a
reassurance and a reminder of my responsibilities. The
beach pebbles were not uncomfortable to my bare feet,
but I avoided prickly bushes. There must be some limit
to the hospitality of this land. When I crossed a little
brook, I knelt and drank some water out of my hands,
less because I was thirsty than for the pure joy of
drinking. The water seemed not like wine—that was
too tame a comparison—but like the essence of all
cool, satisfying drinks.

As I got beyond the low cliff above the beach, I
could see a great mountain high above me. A peaceful
banner of smoke or steam floated from it. I wondered
what the mountain corresponding to it in my world was
doing now. I ran up the slopes and toward the summit
as lightly as I had run the road from Amnisos to N'sos
that night long ago. Somewhere near the top of the
mountain was a flare of red light, barely visible in the
sunlight. Going toward it seemed the right thing to do.
At any rate, there was nowhere else to go; the land was
as empty as the part of the Bright Land I had entered
from Kaphtu.

As I came close to the reddish light I saw outlined
against it a tall, male figure. As I came closer I saw
that his body was magnificently developed, with
massive shoulders and arms and a deep, hairy chest.
The hair and beard were as red as my father's had been
when he was young. But the legs were thin and
somehow wasted, one of them was twisted and

174

deformed. If the one I had met in the court and the sea was Posudi, this could only be Hephaestus. His face when he turned it to me had both lines of strain around the mouth and laughter lines around the eyes. A human face, as Posudi's had not been, but a face of great power, too. A craftsman's measuring eyes, a craftsman's clever fingers. Almost automatically I gave the sign my father had taught me.

He smiled, a gentle smile with a touch of sadness. "Who are you, child?" he asked.

I stood as straight as I could. "My father is Lykos, the craftsman, one of your descendants, Son of Hera. I have my mother's name. I am Britomartis, daughter of Britomartis."

He put his hand on my hair, gently. "Welcome child," he said. "Your mother is greatly loved. Even my own mother is fond of her, which can be said of few. Your father and his cousin Daedalus are known to me. I am proud to call them my sons."

I felt I could trust him. "Grandfather," I said, "I am here because I am worried about the people who live on this island in my world. M'nos is sending ships to bring them off, but will there be time?"

He nodded understandingly. "Look down in the crater, child," he said.

Looking where he pointed I saw that we stood on the edge of an enormous pit, the hollow inside of the great mountain. In its bottom was something molten, brighter than bronze melted in the forge, almost as bright as the sun. The red light came from it, and the steam and smoke I had seen from below came from it.

Hephaestus spoke. "I opened a Path at the right place in the Low World. The melted rock is coming through here, as you can see. For awhile, it will relieve the pressure. But it is only temporary. There are forces too great even for me to handle. Even if I could stop it entirely it would not be wise, it would break out somewhere else. Even this material must return to the Low World eventually; it would disturb Justice to keep it here."

I looked at him. "Justice?" I asked.

He nodded. "You should understand. Pound the metal in at one place, it must come out somewhere else. You can alter the properties of things, but not their natures. For anything to come here permanently from the Low World, something must go there, and for anything from here to go permanently to the Low World something must come here. Justice, balance, necessity, call it what you will. The balance can be changed for awhile. But eventually Justice must be restored. When Cronos came to this world, a balance was upset. When the Others were sent to the Lower World and Cronos and Hades with them, the balance was disturbed much more. Every Path opened is a point of strain. Upset the balance enough and those in the Lower World could possibly return here. They are already active in your world, because Justice has been disturbed. It is sometimes necessary to disturb Justice, but it must be restored. All of us, even Zeus, must serve Justice or we will destroy ourselves."

I felt that in something he had said there was an idea of great importance for me, but I would have to think about that later. At the moment there were several more pressing problems. These Olympians seemed willing enough to do things for you if asked. I determined to try my luck again. "Grandfather," I said, "can you tell me how to move between this world and my own? Each time I've come through from there to here it's been with the help of someone from here." I suppose you could call what Dion had done help. At any rate it had led to this meeting.

Hephaestus bowed his head, considering. When he spoke it was like my father explaining something, patient, precise and practical. "It is hard for us born here to explain," he said. "Because it is easier for us. From here to the Low World is not hard, especially if you focus on a place or person there whom you know or who is thinking of you. That is how we know sometimes that someone in the Low World is calling on us. It creates a sort of pull. If you follow that pull you slip into the Low World. It is always easier near a point of strain; many temples and shrines in the Low World are built at such points. On Kaphtu, for instance, there is a point of strain at N'sos itself and another in a cave near the sea, where they have a port."

I nodded—N'sos where I had entered the Bright Land and Amnisos where I had left it for the first time.

He went on. "Strain points often come in pairs, not too far apart. The Birth Cave on Dicte has a matching strain point at one of the mountain shrines. There are others on Kaphtu, but those two pairs are the most powerful." This was something to remember; my father had suggested that Mother might be somewhere on Mount Dicte. Hephaestus knitted his brows now and spoke more slowly. "From there to here is harder,

177

even for us. The longer you stay, the harder it is. If you carry something from here it helps. That's why Athena sometimes wears a helmet and carries that big shield. She likes to poke around the Low World and interfere, and the helmet and shield hold the power like hot rocks holding the heat." He smiled and I smiled back. This was more than ever like my father, who had used the same metaphor of heat for the power of the Bright Land and had used the homely comparison of the two pots.

He scratched his head. "If I were you, I would try thinking very hard of a place here where you have been. Sometimes it helps to walk a pattern of some sort: a simple spiral will do. But that is simply a way of getting your body to help your mind. The power is really controlled by your thoughts. If you eat or drink here that helps you return. And carrying something from here with you, even something quite small. But do you wish to return to your own land now?"

I nodded reluctantly. "There will be friends of mine who may need help, or if not friends then those dear to my friends. I started off trying to bring a ship here. If I can't do that perhaps there is something I can do."

He smiled warmly. "You are like your mother," he said. "She was always trying to help those on her island and those in Kaphtu who called on her. Some of us think of the power we have been given as a responsibility, and one we may be called to account for."

This was fascinating enough to drive my other concerns from my mind for the moment. "Who can call you to account? Zeus?"

He shook his head. "Not Zeus, son of Cronos—he is just the strongest and wisest of us Olympians. But there is One above us. Call it the King above all the Kings, or call it the Mother of all the Mothers; it has no human form or sex as we have. For a time it has left the power to us—or rather to the Old Ones from whom we got it. But they and we are only stewards and some day there will be a reckoning of our stewardship."

This was too much to take in now; I would have to ponder it. "I'd better go now, Grandfather," I said. "A short time here is a long time in my land."

He nodded. "Yes," he said. "But you can control even that to some extent. Think not only of a place you wish to go but of a time. There are limits. You can't return there before you came here. But within those limits you can return not only to the place but the time you choose. Do you know any person or place on this island?"

I shook my head. "No, or at least perhaps I may. Some of my friends may be here on the ships which have come to help the people here."

He nodded and took my shoulder, turning me toward the sea. "Down there by the cove," he said, pointing, "is the harbor city in your land. This is where the second point of strain is which corresponds to the one here. Look down there and think of your friends. I will give you a little push if you need it, but you may not. And tell the people that there will be time for everyone to be taken off in ships. I promise it."

I smiled at him a little shyly. "Thank you, Grandfather," I said. "Of all of those I have met here you have been kindest to me. I hope we meet again."

179

He chuckled, a deep rumble in which my imagination caught the rumble of the fire-mountain. "We will, child. Oh yes, we will" I looked down toward the empty bay and the land that shelved down toward it and thought of my shipmates. Especially, somehow the thought of Kom'ku came to my mind, Kom'ku harassed and uncertain, thinking of a leader he had trusted. I stared at the bay and suddenly the shapes changed and blurred.

I was standing on a low hill, the bay at my feet. Above me the sky was filled with dust and smoke. The ground beneath me trembled and subsided. There was an acrid odor in my nostrils. The mountain, now high above me, cast a lurid red glow on the low-lying clouds above it. Just below me a panic-stricken crowd was pushing and shoving toward the edge of the water where ships were moored. Many ships but still pitifully few for that great crowd. Above the crowd seemed to hover a misty, dark shape like a great bird, and from that shape dark tentacles descended on the crowd. Wherever they touched, fear became panic and terror; men shouted, women screamed or sobbed, children cried.

The sense of power and well-being that I always had on my returns from the Bright Land was with me and when I saw children pushed and trampled in the panic, anger was added to the power. I pushed with my mind at the dark shape as I might push at a bull out of control: away, out, go! If the thing was a personal being and not just a dark influence it was totally unprepared for my appearance and my attack. It dwindled away and vanished. The crowd was calmer now, but ordinary fear and terror were still present.

I saw that my flesh glowed as it had when I returned the second time from the Bright Land and this gave me an idea. I tried to use my mind to increase that glow, to make myself shine even more brightly. Then I stepped to the brow of the hill.

"Listen," I cried. The cries in the crowd ceased and every eye was fixed on me. "Have no fear," I called down to them. "Your lives are safe. Hephaestus has promised to hold the fire-mountain in check until you are all safely off this island. Send the children with their mothers out to the ships. Let the men and the women without children gather your most precious possessions to be taken with you. Your houses and your land you must bid farewell to, but Hephaestus will not send you forth naked."

Then, as I had sent my powers into the womb of Anadamano's mother in the cave, I tried to send strength and courage into the whole crowd. As they quieted, I could feel the power draining from me and the glow on my skin died, as I remembered how it had died as I healed Anadamano in his mother's body. When I felt drained of power, I stepped back from the brow of the hill and made my way around it to the edges of the crowd. They were quiet and peaceful now—father's kissing children and getting instructions from their wives as to what to bring away, natural leaders in the group beginning to organize squads of men and young women.

As I expected, no one in the crowd paid much attention to me or identified me with the bright figure on the hill. There was an occasional curious glance at my Dancer's kilt as I made my way down to the water's edge. It seemed quite natural to see Kom'ku there, along with a group of sailors who had been trying to keep the crowd from swamping the small boats or trying to swim out to the ships in their panic.

Kom'ku who was wiping blood from a child's knee looked up and recognized me. His face lit up.

"Chryseis!" he cried. "You got a ship in Athens then! The Aeginans were magnificent: we have every ship of theirs that was available. And a shining figure just appeared on the cliff..."

I interrupted. "I heard," I told him. "Things ought to be all right now. It's just a question of ferry service. Is our ship, the one we came from Kaphtu on, still here?"

He nodded. "It will be going soon, now we can load it in an orderly fashion. Do you want to go back to Kaphtu on it?"

I nodded reluctantly. "Since it looks as if things will be all right here, I now have to start thinking about my Dancers and about Ariadne who may be worried about me. I feel guilty about getting away on one of the first ships, but I can help with the children." He smiled and gave me a quick hug. "If anyone deserves a place in the first ship, you do, Chryseis. We owe the Aeginan ships to you, even aside from the ship you brought from Athens." I didn't tell him that I hadn't brought a ship from Athens. But all in all, I thought that perhaps I had deserved a place on a ship to Kaphtu.

Chapter Fifteen: THE WINE SHOP

As it turned out, I went back to Kaphtu on an Aeginan ship. The Aeginan captains had been given some instructions about me by the Temple—certainly not the whole truth but enough to make them very eager to do whatever they could for me. It was really impossible for me to refuse to sail with them without insulting them and it was even a problem which ship to sail on. I left that problem to them, telling them I would go on one of their ships, but that they must choose which. We started in late afternoon and rowed all night raising our sail as the breeze came up with the rising sun. It was a strange but peaceful night: the stars shining above, mothers soothing fretful children, the crew members going quietly back and forth as they took turns at the oars.

Luckily our ship was a wide-beamed merchant vessel, the biggest of the Aeginan ships. The passengers were mostly wives and children of seamen and not frightened of the sea. But the ship was never meant to carry as many people as it was now carrying, and when the children had slept and wanted to move around the ship seemed crowded to bursting. The sailors helped all they could, and a few sensible mothers organized quiet games or storytelling sessions.

As we got closer to Kaphtu the older children hung over the rail, looking at the approaching shore, and had to be watched. A school of dolphins followed us for awhile, and even the smaller children were fascinated by their leaping and playing.

I had been kept busy translating, for though like most traders the Aeginans spoke a little of several languages, their stock of Kaphtui words was not enough to deal with problems involving fretful babies, seasick mothers or lost toys. I was beginning to worry about what would happen to all of our passengers when we arrived in Kaphtu. Most of them had come aboard with only what they had grabbed from their homes when the panic-stricken rush to the harbor began. Some of them had brought treasured possessions or had hastily assembled a bundle of necessities. But one woman was carrying an old empty water pot she had been carrying to the fountain and another had snatched up a basket and filled it with her cosmetics and perfumes. We used the water pot as a slop jar and let some of the children paint themselves with the cosmetics.

I need not have worried about the passengers, for when we arrived at Amnisos there were harbor officials in small boats to lead us to an unloading place on the dock and court ladies directing refugees to temporary housing. Most of them had friends or relatives on Kaphtu who could take them in eventually, but for the moment most of the population of Amnisos had been sent to their friends and relatives inland, and their houses commandeered for housing refugees. I found Ariadne in a small house near the dock, where she was directing the housing of the refugees. We fell into each other's arms despite the curious glances of the officials and refugees standing about clamoring for Ariadne's attention.

She had been worried about me, of course, when she learned from the Athenian novices that I had not returned with the ship, but she had been too busy organizing things to worry much, and besides as she said wryly when we got a moment alone, "It's no use worrying about you, Britomartis. As the sailors say, if you were thrown into a pile of stinking fish, you'd come out smelling like flowers."

I grinned at her. "Farmers have that saying, too," I said. "But they don't say a pile of stinking fish. I've been lucky so far and I've had a lot of help. Speaking of help, what can I do?"

It was mostly translation again, of course, smoothing the way between Kaphtui officials who didn't normally deal with Danaans and Danaan captains from Aegina and from other islands that had sent ships to help. I also ran a good many errands. My Dancer's kilt cleared the way for me and saved questions about who I was and what my authority was. The aura of "children of the King" still hung over the Dancers, and the changeover to the Athenians had not changed that yet. The running around kept me in good condition, and Ariadne told me that I need not worry about the next Dance being scheduled before Dariapana was evacuated.

"M'nos has more things to worry about at the moment than vengeance," she said. "And the Festival of Return will be turned into a Thanksgiving Festival when we have everyone off of Dariapana safely. Besides, M'nos is more like his old self than he has been in years. When we got the news from Dariapana, he threw off his depression and began organizing things. This will be a blow to Kaphtu; trading disrupted, refugees to take care of. Dariapana was becoming a second Kaphtu and I think M'nos had dreams of colonies on the other Circle Islands and even on the mainland. But I'd rather have him dreaming grandiose dreams of that kind than meddling with Those Below. With Astariano gone, maybe M'nos will become himself again."

As soon as we had a little time to ourselves, I had told her what Posudi had told me about her parentage. Surprisingly, this made her more tolerant of M'nos, now that she did not have the guilt of not loving her father as her generous nature told her she should. She could now think of M'nos only as her mother's brother and as the king who, whether we liked him or not, ruled Kaphtu and must be obeyed. My news about my mother was also cushioned for her by the discovery of her own parentage. Late one night as we sat eating a meal there had been no time for all the busy day she laughed and said, "Look at us, Britomartis. A fine pair of demigoddesses we are. Red-eyed, asleep on our feet, our hair in tangles. I haven't had a bath for days."

I laughed in return, yawned and stretched. "Then get yourself to bed," I retorted, "and come swim with me tomorrow morning, before the problems start coming in. I've told you what I've learned and what I've thought. It's the power of that sun in the Bright Land that gives the Olympians their power. A little of that and we could work all day and all night without feeling it." I looked down at her as she sat there, her elbows on the table and her chin on her hands.

"Ariadne, would you really like to be a goddess?" I asked.

"Oh it sounds very wonderful; I don't suppose they age or die, and just living in the Bright Land would be delightful. But what do they do with themselves? They have no need to work or to defend themselves from enemies or to plan for the future. My mother found something to do by taking care of the people of Aegina. but that's like being a queen here. You know well enough that there are more sorrows than joys in that job."

She looked at her hands. "Britomartis, I'll tell you something I've never told anyone else, because you won't misunderstand it. I've never felt at home here in Kaphtu, never really seen myself marrying a Kaphtui and ruling beside him as his queen. I've always envied N'suto who'll grow up to follow in P'sero's footsteps, adventuring and trading in foreign lands. I have no desire to be a man, but I envy them their freedom. Even in Kaphtu, no one would seriously think of a woman commanding a trading ship, or having adventures. The Dance was my adventure for awhile, but once you've mastered it, it becomes just a job like any other. If a goddess is really free, as no woman now is really free, I *would* like to be a goddess."

I nodded slowly. This was an aspect of things I hadn't thought of before and it fitted in very well with my own rebellion against the woman's role they had tried to thrust on me as I was growing up in Athens.

What would I do when my days as a Dancer came to a end. Marry? Become a priestess? Join my father wherever his wanderings had taken him? Being with my father would be wonderful, but in what kind of place would we live? My father, who had stolen a goddess from her temple and married her, neither despised women nor feared them. But he had an unshakable inner security. His own work and his own thoughts were enough for him. He had no need to bolster his own insecurity by putting others below him. But how many men were there like my father? What man who became my husband would still be my friend?

Not Menesthius, despite his many good qualities, and not Glaukos. All of the male Dancers thought of me as a leader, but they did not really think of me as a woman; I did not draw the kind of glances from them that Alceme did. If they did think of me in that way, I knew that even Menesthius would have trouble thinking of me as a leader or even as an equal. Even aside from his age, Daedalus's misogyny was not entirely a pose. P'sero was almost as much a father to me as my own father. Oddly enough, the only man who as a man (setting aside his enmity and his dabbling with the Dark Powers) I could imagine as a husband, out of those I knew, was M'nos himself. On an impulse, I told Ariadne so.

She nodded understandingly. "I can see that. If he had lived up to the best that was in him, he could be a great man. Even as he is he is still a great king. But there is no one like him for either of us to choose as husband." She looked at me mischievously. "You know what the court ladies say about us." We looked at each other and laughed. On some of the Outer Islands, they say the women make love to each other when the men are gone on their long voyages. There were malicious tongues to suggest that my relation to Ariadne was of that kind. We were not shocked at the idea, but it did not interest us either. Those who think all close friendships between women (or between men) must involve physical desire only show their ignorance of friendship.

Gradually the flood of refugees thinned to a trickle—mostly responsible officials who had stayed until the last moment to see that everything worth salvaging on Dariapana had been saved. They told us that the fields and the streets of the town were being buried under the ash from the firemountain and that even on the sea around the island there were great floating masses of ash. Ariadne and I stayed in Amnisos partly to sort out refugees but partly because of a horrified fascination with the fate of Dariapana. It was like being at the bedside of a dying person. You can do nothing for them but somehow cannot bear to leave them and go about your ordinary business.

The port of Amnisos was busier and more variegated than it had ever been. Normally, M'nos discouraged ships from other lands coming to Kaphtu. He wanted trade in his own hands and done by his own ships. But now word had gotten out that captains could earn rich rewards from M'nos by ferrying refugees and their goods from Dariapana to Kaphtu and ships from every port were in Amnisos discharging passengers and cargo before going back for another load. There were so many that they had to he anchored out in the harbor or in other coves up or down the coast. Guards were placed on the streets leading up to the town to keep the foreigners in the dock area, but the dock area itself was so crowded with foreign sailors that the Kaphtui themselves were lost in the crowd.

The great gathering place was the wine shop. Every inhabited place that sailors land they will find a skin or jar full of wine—stealing it if they can, trading for it if they must. Every sailor has a little stock of trinkets to trade with the local people for wine or food or other favors. But in Kaphtu even this little bit of trade is in the hands of palace officials. Sailors must bring their trade goods to a port official. He assesses their value and gives the sailor scraps of parchment or even bits of palm leaves on which symbols have been written, like the symbols on the tablet which had conveyed my flock of sheep to me. Some of these scraps with symbols can be traded for wine in a building on the dock, a little like the guest house at the gates of the House.

The sailors sleep on their ships, of course, but there are rooms in this house on the dock for the captains of trading ships, and food can be traded for or exchanged for the scraps of papyrus or leaf with the appropriate symbols. Local girls in search of adventures with sailors, or presents from them, hang around the place, but they are not allowed in. Ordinarily, it is a fairly quiet and well-behaved place but with all the foreign ships in port it had become very busy and a little disorderly. But there had not been enough problems yet to post a guard there, and so when I passed by late one afternoon and heard the clash of weapons coming from the interior there was no one on the streets to call for aid.

I could have passed by. I had no real responsibility and no authority. But curiosity got the better of me and I pushed aside the reed mat which screened the door and went into the drinking room. Sailors were sitting at the tables, looking at the fight as if it were an entertainment. At the far end of the room, near the heavy high table where the wine was passed out was a man with his back to a corner of the room, sword in one hand and dagger in the other, fighting off three men with swords. He was fighting magnificently and even taunting his attackers between gasping breaths, but I could see that he was tiring and that sooner or later one of his opponents would get under his guard.

He and his attackers were all Danaans, I could tell from their dress and the few words I heard even sounded like Attic speech. This made me feel a responsibility I might not have felt otherwise, and the unfairness of the odds aroused my anger.

"Stop that!" I shouted and took a step toward them. One of the attackers, who seemed to be their leader, jerked his head and another of them came toward me with his sword, a nasty grin on his face.

I was tensing myself for some sort of leap, my mind racing. If I could do a handspring which would end up with my feet in his face could I hurt or disarm him or would he simply spit me on his sword? But I need not have worried. As soon as he started toward me a sailor at a nearby table tripped him up, and another smashed a wine jar on his head. The man behind the wine-serving table, who was a palace servant, produced a thick cudgel from under his table and knocked down one of the remaining assailants. The beleaguered man rushed his remaining opponent who turned to run, tripped and was hit with several wine jars by nearby sailors. Within a moment of my intervention the three attackers were unconscious on the floor and the man they had attacked was standing alone, his chest heaving but with a grin on his face, sheathing his sword and dagger.

"Thanks, friend," he called in Danaan. "Or should I say, 'my Lord,' seeing how these people obey you?" He broke off in astonishment as I came farther into the room. Outlined against the door in my Dancer's kilt, my figure could easily have been that of a slender youth. But as I came closer he could see that I was a woman. We looked at each other for a long moment.

He was not much taller than I, but much broader. His body was seamed with scars and his nose was slightly bent out of line by a blow in some old fight. His eyes were daneing with excitement and I knew he had been enjoying the fight, despite the odds. In spite of the scars and the crooked nose he was a handsome fellow. There was something immediately engaging and attractive about him. But for all that I would have trusted him about as much as I would a wild bull not under my control. It was a completely reckless face. He was young, but you could imagine him having done anything or doing anything. Ariadne had longed for adventure; here was adventure incarnate, and even then I had a twinge of uneasiness at the thought of them together.

For this was plainly not a man with much respect for women. As soon as he saw my sex his smile changed from a friendly grin to an ingratiating smirk and he said in a bantering tone, "Pardon me, my dear. To what do I owe your kind intervention?" He was saying as plainly as if he had said it in words that he thought of women as fools, to be manipulated by a smile and cajoled rather than conversed with.

I looked him coolly in the eye and said in an indifferent voice, "We don't like Athenian corpses cluttering our port." Then I turned to the serving-man behind the wine table and said in Kaphtui, 'Thank you, friend. Will you have these men carried out and thrown in the harbor? That should wake them up. And tell the harbor watch not to let them land again. They can swim to their ship and stay there." He grinned broadly and saluted me, then turned to enlist the help of some others to carry out my order.

I turned back to the benches and found the man who had tripped up the Danaan who had come to attack me and his companion who had brained him with the wine jug. As I thought, they were Aeginans. I held out my hands, and they bowed over them respectfully.

"I'm sorry for the waste of your wine, friends," I said. "Tell the Holy One of Aphea at the temple at home to give you wine for next winter from the temple stocks."

They grinned and imitated the salute the Kaphtui serving man had given me. This was the kind of reward sailors could appreciate.

I lifted a hand in thanks to the others who had helped, but it was for Crooked Nose to reward them if he could; it was his life they had saved. I was turning to go when he spoke again, much more respectfully. "My Lady, I am sorry if my foolish words offended you. From your dress I thought you were a dancer or entertainer here. I thank you for my life and offer you my service." There was still some calculation behind this, no doubt; he did not want to offend someone important, and the actions of the serving man and the sailors showed I was that. But there was honest regret and honest gratitude in his tone too, and I liked him better for his apology.

I smiled at him a little more warmiy and said, "I am a dancer of sorts, but I dance with the bull, for the god. Give your thanks to the men who helped you. All I did was call out. Why did the men attack you?"

He answered evasively. 'They are kinsmen of mine, Lady, it is a family quarrel. I do thank these men, and I will reward them, but if it had not been for you they would not have helped me—it was none of their quarrel. I have never heard of dancing with a bull. I would like to see that."

I considered. There was no absolute prohibition against foreigners at the Dance—it was rather that M'nos controlled very carefully what strangers came to the palaces, or anywhere inland. This man's hair was as dark as Ariadne's, though his eyes were green. He could pass as a Kaphtui, if he was careful.

I told him, 'The Dance will be danced tomorrow at N'sos. If you can make your way there, you may see it. Be careful how you behave-Athenians are not popular with King M'nos. Farewell, I have preparations to make." I nodded and walked out the door, feeling his eyes on me. It was true enough that I had preparations to make; the time I had spent at Amnisos had lost me practice time. If we had not worked together so much last year, I could not have left my Dancers to practice alone so much. With Ariadne and me both busy, T'ne had been drilling them and doing my leaps, as well as starting the new Athenian novices on their practice with the aid of Alceme, Menesthius and Glaukos.

When I did get back to N'sos the practice run-through went smoothly; it was as if I had never been away. I found the new Athenian novices regarding me with awe: I suspected the others had been using my name to impress them, as nurses use the names of gods and demons to impress children. The only one who made much immediate impression was Menesthius's cousin, Artimodorous, who we hoped would be the tauromath of the group. When I came on to the practice field he was standing at Baby's side, with his arm over his back, Baby sensed my presence immediately and trotted over to me; Artimodorus looked at me with a startled expression and our eyes met. I knew he recognized me as the one who had chosen the novices in Athens. But he said nothing, only greeting me with a shy smile; unlike the others he did not seem in awe of me.

He was a gangling youth and would need a lot of practice to be a Leaper, but his power over animals was great enough to make up for that. The girls, having been selected with some knowledge of their characters rather than on the basis of Aegeus's spite, were a much better group than ours had been and there were several possible Leapers. Alceme, their old ringleader from childhood days, had them well in hand, and I was content to leave them to her. Menesthius and Glaukos had their eyes on a number of potential Leapers among the boys.

So as we prepared for the great Thanksgiving Dance at the postponed Homecoming Festival our troubles once more seemed to be over. In this we were both right and wrong. The old dangers, from the Dance and from the enmity of M'nos, were indeed over, at least for a time. But new and unexpected dangers were ahead, brought upon us by actions that seemed trivial at the time. I was often to wonder in later years what would have happened to us all if I had never passed the wine shop that day, or had passed it by on the other side and not stopped.

Chapter Sixteen: THE GODDESS

The crowd at the Dance was tremendous and somehow I was not surprised when after we had finished I saw on the fringes of the crowd my friend, Crooked Nose, from the wine shop. He was wearing a Kaphtui kilt and was with a man I recognized as a minor official from the port, whom he must have bribed or cajoled into bringing him to N'sos for the Dance. As the crowd thinned, Crooked Nose made his way over to me and imitated the salute he had seen given to me in the wine shop. "My admiration, Lady" he said. "Even among the Amazons I have not seen a woman who could do what you do."

My curiosity was aroused: I had often been called a wild Amazon by the Athenian women, and had wondered if they were real or fabulous. But Crooked Nose did not look like a man who needed to tell tall tales or boast of imaginary exploits, and I asked, "Have you seen the Amazons then? What are they like? Do they really fight like men?"

He grinned. "Yes, Lady, and mostly look like men too, all except a few." His face closed in and there was pain in his eyes. "My first love was a princess of the Amazons," he said. "No woman and no friend has compared with her since. She was killed by her own

197

people because she had broken her vows to Artemis. But our child still lives and is being brought up in safety." He looked me straight in the eyes. "I haven't taken women very seriously since my Hippolyta died, Lady. Perhaps I haven't dared to. But you and your little blonde friend have my respect. I can see you have the bull under some kind of spell. But even so, one slip on those horns... I'm not sure I could do it."

This man would never really be as candid as he appeared to be now, but even so I liked him a great deal better for that speech. And despite his words he was longing to try the Dance, I could see it in his eyes. I don't know if what I said was responsible for what came later. Likely enough he would have had the idea on his own. My words were a jest, intended to bridge the embarrassment of his talk of the love he had lost. "Well, you're a bit long in the tooth, but perhaps King Aegeus will send you to us with the next batch of novices. Then you can try dancing with the bull."

He laughed but I could see that what I had said had not been taken as a jest. "Perhaps he will. Lady. But now I must return to my ship. Farewell." And he melted into the crowd again.

He was no Dion to mingle with the crowd at the party without being noticed and neither Ariadne nor the other Dancers saw him before he left. In the next few days the foreign ships left Amnisos and there were no more Danaan faces on the streets of Amnisos. Crooked Nose soon faded from my mind. Anyhow, I soon had more urgent things to think of. The day after the Dance, M'nos sent for me again, and we had an interview that sent me away with my head whirling. It began tamely enough with some compliments on my handling of the Dancers and on my own performance. Then he gave me the first surprise.

"If you will. Lady," he said, "the new Athenians may be worked into the Dance as soon as they are ready. To ask you and your first companions to serve a year and a half would not be just." No word of the justice of his attempts to use the Dance to kill us, but in a way it was an oblique apology. He went on. "There is something to be said for the Leapers starting off with a bull already used to the Dance before they catch their own. And I do not believe this violates the traditions of the Dance." I nodded. The offer was tempting; until I was free of my responsibility for the Dance I could do little about searching for my mother. And whether M'nos knew it or not the novices would be almost as safe with Baby as my own Dancers, given Artimodorous's power over animals.

"I will consider the idea carefully, my Lord," I said. "And if they are ready by midsummer I may do as you suggest The Dance is a great responsibility and I will not be sorry to lay the burden down."

He nodded and took over the conversation smoothly. "You have borne the responsibility well, Lady, and that has given me an idea. Hear me, but do not answer now, not until you have pondered well what I have to say. My sister-wife gave me no children of my own. Even Andaroko…" Neither his voice nor his face changed but I could feel his pain as he stopped for a moment. "But I have reason to believe that she was sterile with me by her own will and by arts she knew. She wanted to marry another man, but my father insisted that I be M'nos. This was her revenge. Andaroko was her first lover's son, and she swore that Ariadne and Astariano were god's children. But I have reason to be sure I can give children to other women."

Was that true, I wondered, or had some paramour deceived him when she saw he was frantic to prove his virility? At any rate what had this to do with me? I soon found out. "Ariadne's husband will be M'nos after me. That is our law and I do not dispute it. But we have the power and the wealth to found new colonies. Indeed those from Dariapana cannot readily be kept on Kaphtu. I am not too old to have sons still, and my sons may make settlements that can grow to be lands as great as Kaphtu itself. Since my sons will rule new lands, I need not worry about Kaphtui customs. Of all the women I have seen, you are the one most fitted to be a queen. Your blood is royal. There is no other man in Kaphtu worthy of you. Together we could rule Kaphtu for many years and our children could reign in other lands."

He lifted his hand, "Do not speak now, Lady. The idea is strange to you. You will need time to get used to it. When you have had time to think, you will see that this is what must be." I bowed my head and rose to my feet, trying to keep my face impassive. But he had one last thunderbolt to hurl at me. "I think I will marry Ariadne to P'sero's son N'suto. That family is a strong bulwark of our kingdom," he said in a voice so offhand I nearly lost my temper and flared out at him. "And the boy is… a good lad," he went on in a curious tone. An easily controlled puppet I was sure he meant, but there was something else too. With a tremendous effort I kept my self-control and left the room with apparent calm.

There was no Ariadne in her veil waiting for me but I stormed up to her room and found her there quarreling amiably with Alceme. The two had become friends of a sort at last, but there was always a little real edge to their banter. I poured out my news helter-skelter, and it wasn't until I saw the pinched look of misery on Alceme's face that I thought of how M'nos's plans would affect her. Apparently she really loved N'suto after all despite her affectation of contempt. I had never loved Ariadne so well as when she took Alceme into her arms and comforted her.

"Don't worry, Alceme," she soothed. "Even if I were willing to take N'suto from you, which of course, I'm not, N'suto would never hear of it. And P'sero would back him up. M'nos thinks that everyone is like himself and that P'sero would jump at the chance to have a son on the throne and that N'suto would give up anything to be king. You know P'sero and N'suto better than that. Anyway, they're both in Egypt until the end of summer and long before then we'll be in hot water because Britomartis will have refused to become my stepmother." She grinned at me over Alceme's head on her shoulder.

I grinned back. "It would almost be worth it to have you under my thumb, young lady. But Ariadne, is M'nos mad, do you think?"

She shook her head and looked thoughtful.

Alceme wiped her eyes and resumed her usual facade of cynicism. She was the first to speak. "It's as Ariadne said, Chryseis, he thinks everyone is like himself. He thinks you'll jump in bed with a man old enough to be your father in order to be queen, and he thinks Ariadne would marry N'suto so as not to spoil your chances and so that you'll be together. Actually, if you could stand him it wouldn't be a bad idea. You and Ariadne would be the real rulers, whatever M'nos thinks."

Ariadne signaled the resumption of normal relations by snapping at her. "Don't be a fool, Alceme. Do you think I'd let Britomartis marry a man who meddles with the Powers Below, no matter what advantages there were to it?" She went on in a softer tone. "Besides, neither of us has given up on finding a man who we'll feel about us as you feel about N'suto, though it took all this to make you show your feelings. I hope you've let N'suto know how you really feel about him; he won't put up with being treated as you treat him forever." There was one thunderbolt of surprise left for that day.

Alceme smiled her secretive smile and said simply, "Oh. he knows how I feel all right. You'd better take M'nos up on his offer about the new Athenians, Chryseis. I have a feeling that I might be carrying N'suto's child."

After that, of course, there was no choice but to break in the novices as quickly as possible. Alceme had slept with N'suto before he had left for Egypt on his father's ship. That was only a month ago, and she had only missed one period, but Ariadne and I had little doubt that she was right. We put about the story that Alceme had hurt her wrist in practice, and she Danced no more from then on. A tall, dark girl named

Helena, the best of the novices and an old ally of Alceme's, took her place in the next Dance. There were no more triple head leaps, of course; she was not ready for that yet, but she was good for a novice and the crowd was friendly to her and had sympathetic cheers for Alceme when she appeared on the sidelines with a bandaged wrist.

Artimodorus was the next to come into the Dance, taking Glaukos's place. He was still a little clumsy, but he could easily do the Roll Under which had been Glaukos's speciality, for he could sense Baby's movements as well as I could, and Baby would no more have stepped on him than he would have stepped on me. Soon after, one of the other Athenian boys, an outstanding athlete, became good enough to step into Menesthius's place. There we stuck for awhile for none of the other girls was as good as Helena and if I were replaced there would be no one who could do the more spectacular leaps.

I was content to leave it so for awhile, for as long as I was Dancing, M'nos did not press his curious suit. We had expected protests from Alceme about her replacement, but from the moment she was sure she was pregnant she lost her interest in the Dance. She grew better natured and dreamier and spent more time in Psero's house in Amnisos with Riamare and M'pha. She and Ariadne were now genuinely fond of each other and their bickering was purely a matter of form. I hardly recognized in Alceme now the minx who had been so spiteful on the ship from Athens. But there were flashes of the old Alceme, and I think if anyone had threatened her child she would have killed them with the same skill and calmness with which she had leaped the bull.

Eventually, however, one of the new Athenian girls was ready. In fact, several more were almost ready and with more work this group of Dancers might have eight Leapers, like Ariadne's old team. Artimodorus had discovered how to do a head leap by making Baby do most of the work; the bull almost picked Artimodorus up and tossed him over his back. Artimodorus's slight awkwardness made this look more dangerous than it was, and the crowds loved it. Soon Helena was doing head leaps, nothing fancy but neat and well executed. There came a day when I did my last Dance with Baby, and turned over responsibility for the Dance to Artimodorus. I put everything I had learned that year into my last performance. It is still remembered by those who saw it and tall tales are told about it by those who didn't.

I had worked out what I must do after that day. I saw M'nos briefly and told him I was going up to the shrine of Aphea on Mount Dicte to meditate on his offer. He agreed immediately; it is a common thing for Kaphtui women to seclude themselves in this way for a time before marriage. Ariadne accepted another invitation to Ph'stos; Alceme and Riamare went with her; no word of Alceme's condition would reach M'nos from across the mountains. Menesthius and Glaukos stayed as trainers to the new group and T'ne came out of retirement to help them. She had not married; I think she understood bulls better than she understood men. But I saw Menesthius's eyes resting on her sometimes and I had hopes for something in that direction. They would suit each other, both being quiet, sweet-natured people who might be taken advantage of by more selfish spouses. Glaukos had finally given up his calf-love for me and was enjoying the attentions of the female hangers-on of the Dance.

So when I rode out of N'sos on the same donkey I had ridden on my last trip to the hills, I was light-headed with freedom from responsibility. My friends were not worrying about me, but most of all no one was depending on me. Even if I died or ran away, no one would be injured; no Dance would fail, no companions be threatened. I suddenly realized that every moment since the day I had landed in Kaphtu I had been responsible for the lives and welfare of others. I did not regret it and knew I would take such responsibility again, but for now it was wonderful to be free.

Furthermore, I was in no danger myself until I was finally forced to give M'nos a straight answer. Of course, it would have to be a refusal and his fury would be redoubled; against me and possibly against the Athenians again. But while he thought I would accept him all the power that had threatened me was bent to my protection. Even his allies Below would hold their hands if he had any power over them.

As I approached the shrine my mood grew quieter. Underlying all my other problems had been my longing for my mother, and I was now about to put to the test the only scheme I had been able to devise to make contact with her. If that failed I would not know what to do. The site of the shrine was spectacular: high rocky walls that seemed to grow out of the mountains themselves, mountain goats visible on nearby crags. But inside the walls I might almost have been in the Temple on Aegina. I knew the right words to say and the right request to make. I was a suppliant for an appearance of the goddess, with the proper credentials and passwords.

Presently I was left alone in a bare, simple room, with a simple table and chair. Soft chanting began in another part of the shrine and I watched the massive stone door at the other side of the room, unbearable tension building up within me. The door had been very slightly ajar; the most any ordinary suppliant could expect was a light beyond it and a voice. But with the aid of a chair and my Dancer's muscles I had levered it open until it was just possible to slip inside it. As I expected there was nothing beyond it but a shallow stone niche, dusty and bare. I now sat on the battered chair, waiting for something to happen.

The room darkened but as the chant went on a light began shining through the partly open door. As I had suspected, it was the clear golden light of the Bright Land and where it shone on the floor and the table they seemed to become more real, more beautiful, more there. The rest of the room seemed insubstantial.

When the light seemed to be growing no brighter, I leaped for the door, going through the gap with a twist to the right. For a second the light dazzled me, then I saw a tall figure before me. For a moment my heart stopped with hope, but as I looked from the familiar chin to the face above it, I saw that it was older and far sterner than my mother's face. I was in the Bright Land, standing on a rocky peak with the mountains around me, and the stern face before me was the face of an angry and outraged goddess to whom I was merely an impudent intruder.

Luckily, she spoke before blasting me. I realized later how close my escape was. Her words were in an archaic form of Kaphtui and had a ring of ritual: "Who are you that dares to walk the Crooked Ways?"

I drew myself up and looked her in the eye. "Britomartis, daughter of Britomartis, called Aphaea and Chryseis. I am here to find my mother." I paused and then, greatly daring, went on, "Who is, I think, your sister, Lady Athena."

I held my breath, but the moment of crisis had passed. There was a faint smile on those familiar-unfamiliar features and her tone was milder than her words as she replied, "I believe you, impudent child. You resemble my headstrong sister both in face and in folly." She paused, considering. "What powers have you, child, aside from the power to sneak into this world and survive?"

I looked into those gray-green eyes so like my own and answered truthfully, "The power to see what is really there, to see no illusions."

She nodded. "The blessing and the curse of the daughters of Metas," she said. Then she frowned, "What is there about you that makes me think of gryphons?" she asked.

There was no point in concealing anything from her. "I bear a token from Gyros, lord of the gryphons. He has helped me twice and I can call on him once more." Her face showed nothing, but I thought she was impressed. "Treasure that token," she said laconically.

"But there is something else: ah, the little bauble at your throat. You will need that no more for controlling beasts; your powers have grown. Better leave it here; if it were taken from you, it could be used against you."

I was not sure how far I trusted her, but at least that far. I held it out to her. "Will you have, Aunt?" I asked.

She took it from me and her eyes lit up as she saw the workmanship. "Daedalus?" she asked, and I nodded. She tucked it into her sash. She was dressed more or less in Danaan style but the material was even finer than that of my mother's dresses. "I will keep it for you," she said. "Since you have worn it I can use it as a link between us."

She looked at me sternly, but I was already beginning to suspect that her bark was worse than her bite, at least for me.

"Your mother has defied Zeus and she has been placed in the Birth Cave until she comes to her senses. Since it is guarded by the Flying Serpents not even I could get to her. And the Path from that Cave to the Low World is dreadfully guarded. Zeus has always been afraid someone would use the power of the Cave against him. So you might as well return to your own world for now; there is nothing we can do until she changes her mind or Zeus relents. I might be able to change his mind, if I chose to."

I was beginning to lose my fear of her and I flared up at this. "If you chose to! Don't you want your sister to be free?"

Her eyes blazed and if my own temper had not been aroused I would have stepped back from her fury. "Free!" she said bitterly. "Free to do what? To die, to grow old? She wants to join your father in the Low World, to live as a mortal woman. And she would die, she would age: her power would fade. I love her, should I free her to kill herself?"

I saw the pain in her face, and the words "I love her" pulled at my heart. I replied much more gently. "That is her choice, Aunt. If you love her you must respect her decision. But what do the other immortals care if she makes that choice?"

Athena replied with scorn in her voice but nevertheless speaking to me more as an equal. "You don't understand our problems. There are only a few of us, holding this Land and yours against Those Below. We are fertile enough with mortals, but almost none of the children could live in this land. The Old Ones have gone away from us, and with each other we seem to produce no children, except for Zeus. And what have he and Hera produced? Ares!" There was indescribable contempt in her voice.

I looked her in the eyes and spoke softly. "I can live in this land." Those gray-green eyes so like mine held my eyes as she turned this over in her mind. She came to the right conclusion as I knew she would. Here was someone whose mind worked like mine. "You are thinking of an exchange," she said in a tone that was almost awed.

I nodded. "My mother's heart is with my father. If you keep her here by force she'll be of little use to you. If Zeus will take me in her place I'll do whatever I can to help you. I've seen a little of Those Below and I don't like what I've seen. Hephaestus told me that a balance must be preserved. If something from here goes to our world, something from our world should come here. I'm that something."

I literally held my breath while she thought. If I could get this formidable being on my side my mad plan might have some hope of success. When she spoke her voice showed she was half convinced. "But he won't take you seriously if you just make the proposal. If you could show that you have real power, though…" I pulled the gryphon feather from my hair and and let it wind around my finger. "What if I rescue my mother from the cave?" I said.

Suddenly she laughed, an unexpectedly musical sound. Her face looked younger too, without its stern look. "I can't resist someone who uses her mind," she said. "I've helped some sorry rogues because they were clever. Your plan is just audacious enough and unexpected enough, which is only to say mad enough, to succeed. It seems I must lose a sister and gain a niece. If you succeed, bring 'Phaea here. This Path belongs to her temple and she can use it as a refuge. I'll negotiate with Zeus for you. But I can't help you free her."

I nodded. This was as much as I had hoped for and more. If I was going to do this, I had better do it quickly before something or someone interfered. I let the golden feather drift from my fingers. From somewhere in the distance a bright speck appeared and grew larger. There was a sound of mighty wings and the great gryphon swooped down to land before me. There was now no sign of the feather and I felt a sort of vulnerability without it.

The golden eyes flicked over to Athena once, then fixed themselves on mine. I spoke slowly and carefully. "For the last help you promised to give me, I ask you to rescue my mother from the Birth Cave and bring her here." The strange remote voice spoke formally. "Do you lay this task on me by virtue of my promise to you?"

I looked into those strange eyes. "Yes," I said.

"Then I must obey," said the creature.

Was I mistaken or was there the faintest hint of humor in that inhuman voice? He leaped into the air and the great wings beat. Then he gave a high fierce cry and from every corner of the sky other gryphons came winging toward him. Some either had no ears or their ears were folded back: I wondered if these were females.

Athena held my arm and pointed. "We can see the Cave from here," she breathed. "High up the slopes, that dark patch."

I remembered Hephaestus's words: 'The points of strain come in pairs, not far apart." I strained my eyes toward the cave entrance and somehow the scenes became not only clearer but nearer. I wondered if it was Athena's hand on my arm or my own awakening powers.

From in front of the cave, out of the bushes and undergrowth rose serpents like the one Gyros had killed. There was a cloud of them, like a swarm of bees. But the great flight of gryphons arrowed toward the cave, biting and snapping at the serpents if they came too near. Gyros in the center was completely protected from the serpents. The serpents would have been formidable adversaries for any ordinary beast or bird, but the gryphons simply dove through them, scattering them as a hawk scatters pigeons. In the air, the gryphons had the advantage for they could twist and maneuver and batter with their great wings. The serpents could do little more than hover and try to strike. One managed to coil itself around a small gryphon's leg but was plucked off and crushed by the beak of another gryphon.

My heart beat violently when Gyros landed at the entrance to the cave. Surely some of the serpents would be lurking in the rocks. Alter what seemed only a moment he sprang into the air again—had he been driven off? He flew toward us, straight as an arrow; was that something on his back or not? As he cleared the rocks around the cave I heard a high, sweet voice singing. Somehow I was sure it was the same voice I had heard when I first stepped into the Bright Land. The serpents did not pursue, they seemed somehow confined to a certain area around the cave. One or two hurled themselves at the gryphons as they flew away, but their wings fluttered and failed as they reached some invisible barrier. The swarm of serpents descended back to the ground, like bees who have driven off an intruder from their hive.

Gyros's shadow covered us as he circled for a landing. I stood there with my nails biting into the palms of my clenched fists until I saw a figure slip from the back of the great gryphon. This time it was the right figure, the right face. I flew into the arms that I had longed for for eight lonely years. Those arms enfolded me and our tears of joy mingled as a well remembered voice murmured as it had on our parting, "Britomartis—my brave girl."

And that was the end of my quest, and the beginning of my new life.

Richard Purtill

About the Author

Richard Purtill is Professor Emeritus of Philosophy at Western Washington University, and the author of nineteen published books, including six fantasy and science fiction novels. He has made more than twenty visits to Greece, and lived several years in England. His stories have been published in *The Magazine of Fantasy and Science Fiction*, *Isaac Asimov's Science Fiction Magazine*, *Marion Zimmer Bradley's Fantasy Magazine*, *Alfred Hitchcock's Mystery Magazine*, and *The Year's Best Fantasy Stories*.

He is a popular presenter at conferences and conventions, and has been guest of honor at Mythcon in San Diego. He is a member of Science Fiction and Fantasy Writers of America, the Author's Guild, and the National Writer's Union.

Printed in the United States
991300001B